CW01464680

# AT WHAT COST

## By

## Adam Holdsworth

Grosvenor House
Publishing Limited

All rights reserved
Copyright © Adam Holdsworth, 2024

The right of Adam Holdsworth to be identified as the author of this
work has been asserted in accordance with Section 78
of the Copyright, Designs and Patents Act 1988

The book cover is copyright to Adam Holdsworth

This book is published by
Grosvenor House Publishing Ltd
Link House
140 The Broadway, Tolworth, Surrey, KT6 7HT.
www.grosvenorhousepublishing.co.uk

This book is sold subject to the conditions that it shall not, by way of
trade or otherwise, be lent, resold, hired out or otherwise circulated
without the author's or publisher's prior consent in any form of
binding or cover other than that in which it is published and
without a similar condition including this condition being
imposed on the subsequent purchaser.

This book is a work of fiction. Any resemblance to
people or events, past or present, is purely coincidental.

A CIP record for this book
is available from the British Library

ISBN 978-1-80381-915-0

# CHAPTER 1
# HEADACHE

The bottom of my navy denim jeans contrasted nicely with the white leather of my trainers. Or should I say ex white trainers. Mud splats flicked across the front of them, from my slip earlier, which had now ruined them as far as I could tell. One of those slips that catch you off guard, when your foot goes off sideways from your direction of travel. In that split second you fear that you're going to fall and never stop, until you hit the earth's core. Then suddenly it's not so bad. Your foot only travelled about six inches, and you don't actually fall at all. Just left with a raging heartbeat and another new pair of trainers (that you promised your wife you'd keep clean) virtually ruined. Stumbling over the little green metal bridge trying my hardest not to look drunk, when I clearly am. In my mind, I could hold a clear conversion with the Prime Minister. When in reality, I'm going from side to side with each step I take and praying I don't see anyone that I know.

The engine rumbling at the bus stop directly below my bedroom window is my cue to attempt the first eye open of the day. Only slightly at first, feeling that unwelcome burn from the sun on my pupils. Eyes closed again, for safety. The realisation is beginning to take hold of me. My head feels like it's full of concrete and that awful taste in my mouth from the (God knows how much) beers I had to drink with my old school pals last night at the Odd Fellows Arms. Second attempt to open my eyes was a success. I need to keep them open and I'm sure at some point the burn will stop, but it doesn't stop yet.

One last roll under the covers confirms what I already knew but didn't want to accept. That I've slept in. Beth normally wakes up around 9 o'clock on a Sunday, or at least gets out of bed then. My outstretched arm would normally land on her upper thigh and feel the warmth glowing from the woman I love and married five years ago. However, my hand only landed on the flat, empty side of the sheets. In a daze, I waved my hand up and down across the cotton. Hoping to find her still laying there. Perhaps she had shrunk down. But no. The bed was empty, except from a still slightly drunk me, who at this point was becoming filled with self-pity for my impending doom of a hangover, which will last for the day, but feel like an eternity.

That bus driver must know what he is doing. Revving the engine in perfect unison, with every time a lightning bolt of pain hits my temples. It sounds like he's completed his formation lap and waiting for the green light at the end of so many reds to start the Grand Prix. I throw off the covers and roll out of bed, my feet hitting the soft carpet. My hands rubbing at my eyes, trying desperately to stop them burning. Looking sorrowful at my pile of last night's clothing. Instantly thinking, I'm going to need to put those in the washing basket or not only will I have the hangover, but also a moody wife for a day and I can't deal with both. In that split second, I'm hit with a flash back from last night. I often forget a lot of the previous evening, where alcohol is involved, so these little half memories help me piece the night together.

*Walking dead straight (stumbling from side to side, like a lost crab) up the driveway. Trying to summon my inner stealth, ninja like skills of silence. A huge flash of light hit me. Spinning around on the block paving, looking up for the helicopter overhead and realising that it was the security light that had come on above the garage door and not some commando team, in a chopper trying to take me out.*

*Stumbling and fumbling for my keys. Looking down and saying out load, "These trainers are fucked, Beth*

3

*will kill me". They are a lot worse than I thought on the bridge, especially now that the light has hit them. I had the sudden urge to discard the evidence. Maybe throw them straight in the bin. However, Beth might be even more mad if she thinks I've walked home in my socks and will come to her own conclusion, that I'd fallen asleep somewhere and had them stolen. A plan formed in my head. To jet wash them, first thing in the morning, before she woke.*

*With the front door key finally located, I always put it in the little pocket, above the normal pocket on the right side of my jeans. It still took me a good ten minutes to find them. While I'm trying the lock, I look up and realise that our bedroom window was illuminated. I'm praying that she's fallen asleep with the light on. A quick glance at my watch, 12:17am. It's taken me thirty minutes to walk (stumble) one and a half mile. The front door finally opens, I close it with complete silence (in my head anyway). All locked back up. I strip out of my clothes in the passageway, stumbling with one leg in and one leg out of my Levi's, nearly knocking over the vase that's standing proudly on the radiator cover. Both legs now free from there denim constraints. Socks and underwear follow suit. Fumbling around in the dark, I try to locate the downstairs bathroom. Once I finally located it, I had quick pee and then tried to wash my hands and face. If she is still awake, I needed to look at least a little fresh.*

*Picking up my pile of clothes, while leaving my ruined trainers in the passageway. I make the slow and steady ascent up the stairs. I can hear vague voices. She must have left the tv on too. As I creep further the up the wooden hill, I realise that it's Beth's voice I can hear. I can't make out any of the words or at least not in my flashback, but it's 100% her talking. I approach the door, avoiding the squeaky floorboard in the centre of the landing and her voice quietens. I wait for a moment. When I turn the handle and enter our bedroom the light is off and I can just make out her silhouette, laying on her side and seemingly sleeping. "Are you awake?". I received no reply.*

I put both hands on my knees and make the awkward attempt to stand up. Successfully on the first attempt. Today maybe a good day. I throw on the robe that was hanging from the back of our bedroom door, looking like a washed up, drunk Obi Wan Kenobi. Grabbing the pile of clothing from the floor, and getting that nostril hit of spilt, stale beer radiating from them and make the slow, painful walk across the landing to the bathroom, again avoiding the squeaky floorboard, to discard of them into the washing basket abyss. Not before separating them into lights and darks. Another win with the wife. After a burning pee, I slowly make the descent down the stairs, awaiting whatever punishment my wife has in store.

She was sitting reading the paper at the breakfast bar, also wrapped in her robe, looking like she was at a spa. Lilly must have gotten out of bed a lot earlier than me to deliver the paper. Lilly was our paper girl, very sweet and always polite. Beth's parents had called us posh for getting the newspaper delivered. But in reality, it was only because we normally liked to lounge around on Sundays and not having the hassle of getting dressed to go and pick the paper up, it was well worth the extra one pound for this convenience. Beth had the coffee machine set up ready for me to use. As I entered, she glanced up from the paper and looked at me with dead eyes. I thought, now I'm about to get wrong. But her face turned from this to a beautiful smile, a smile I hadn't seen in a long time. "Good night then?" she said. And I responded with "Yeah it was, from what I can remember". Her eyes rolled and she jumped off the stool and headed over to make me a coffee. "I have to get sorted and dressed soon, I need to nip over and see my mam for a few hours" she said while not looking away from the coffee machine.

"Didn't you go and see her yesterday? All afternoon, actually." I said, with a hint of suspicion in my voice.

"Yeah, but I just need to see her again, also it will give you the chance to sober up and have a shower or whatever. Also, Mr! I've cleaned those trainers and they're outside drying". She seems overly bright when I was expecting a stern telling off.

"Thanks" I returned. "Can you not go and see her another day? I want to curl up on the sofa with you" "Sorry honey, I need to go today. Here's your coffee, hopefully it will work a miracle and sober you up" She laughed and headed to the passageway, but before she got through the door I said, "Who were you speaking to last night when I got home?"

"Oh, not this again, I was asleep when you came home, now I've got to go and get dressed" she said, seeming a little annoyed. With that she left.

Why was she lying or was it me? Had I just made the whole thing up out of paranoia from the past? She had cheated before, with a colleague from work. Could that be back on? My mind races when I think about her past indiscretions, and she lied about it before too. I always refer to it as her indiscretion, it helps me not to think about it in detail and sort of makes it sound not so bad. I need to clear my head, this hangover isn't helping either. As I sip at my coffee and contemplate what I might do for the rest of the day, I gaze out of the window and see my trainers hanging by their laces from the washing line, swaying to and throw from the breeze like clackers. Brilliantly white, she had done a good job on those. But why did she do it? She's never done that before. Normally I would have to sort it out myself or at least I'd get a mouth full from her about wasting money on clothes and ruining them because I can't handle my drink. So why now and why this morning? Is it her guilt maybe? God, I need to get my head out of this. And the plans I put in place last night with Connor might help me find out.

I heard the quick steps come down the stairs. Keys jingling in the bowl. And "All sorted, be back in a few hours!" was shouted through the house. Then the front door opened and slammed shut. She had never been able to just close the door. It had to be slammed as she leaped through it. I could hear the faint engine noise as her car started up and, in an instant, it was silence again.

My coffee was working a little. I even had a little walk around the garden, checking on the grass I'd cut the day before, just in case it had grown any in the twenty-four hours that had passed. With my cup now empty, I was at a crossroads. Do I make another cup of coffee and sit where Beth had been seated to read the newspaper and find out which celebrity was cheating on their partner or go and jump in the shower to try and freshen up? Option two had won the mental battle, after much internally deliberation about having to get dressed after the shower, but I thought it might help me feel a little more normal. Walking through the passageway I noticed another parcel all wrapped up ready to be delivered. "What the hell is she selling now?" escaped my lips to the empty house. Buying new and selling old clothes had become quite a regular thing for Beth over the last few weeks. I had noticed my credit card taking a hit for her new clothes. It did worry me a little that, she bought new clothes on my card but when she sold old ones the money went into our joint account. She had a bad credit rating from an old loan she had, and the bank wouldn't let her get a credit card. So, she convinced me to get one for her to use and promised to take care of the bills etc.

The ascent up the stairs was a lot more of a success story than the previous evenings attempt. Walking into the bathroom and turning on the over bath shower for it to warm up. I stood staring at myself in the mirror. Noticing the red eyes first and praying that they return to white soon. I also noticed how old I was looking this morning. Thirty-seven going on fifty-seven, slightly greying hair and more wrinkles appearing by the minute. Praying that the shower would help. But having the realisation that it's only hot water and not the fountain of youth. Maybe this is why Beth's straying? Jesus, I've confirmed her as guilty without knowing anything remotely close to the facts yet. As I disrobed and got under the water, I instantly felt better. Even if it's only for the next five minutes, it was totally worth it. I lathered up my head with shampoo and as the water cascaded over my hair to rinse the sudds from it. The water went cold. Only for a few seconds. "What's wrong with the boiler now!" I said out loud, again to an empty audience. I stopped washing for a few moments. Something about the word "Wrong" had me thinking, Deep thinking. Why that word? What does it have anything to do with anything? Then it hit me. The previous evening as I approached our bedroom door and could hear Beth's voice, I can now remember what I heard. I couldn't make out much of it, but I do remember a broken sentence. "..........Done, It's.............. Wrong.........". maybe she was only having a moment of weakness and telling whoever was on the other end of the phone "I'm done, it's over, it was wrong". I'll need the proof from Connor.

Shower complete and my mind racing once more. I don't plan on leaving the house today, so I throw the robe back on and head downstairs to the kitchen. Time for another coffee, I'm not in the right frame of mind to go through the process of using the filtered coffee machine. So, I resort to the old-fashioned way of instant coffee. The kettle seeming to take an age to fill and feels too heavy. God, I drank too much last night if I'm not physically able to lift the kettle. The struggle is almost over as it lands on the stand, and I click the button down. Feeling content that the little orange light came on. It should be boiled soon. I grab my favourite mug, the biggest in the cupboard and drop one and half teaspoons of fancy instant coffee in. We can afford the good stuff these days. I waddle over to the fridge barefoot because I forgot that my slippers are upstairs and there's no way I'm walking back up those anytime soon. Now with the fridge open and milk collected. I hadn't made it over to my mug before the beep of the fridge let me know that the door was left open. I quickly pour a little in the mug and rushed over to put the milk back, just so that the beeping would stop. The kettle clicked and the orange light was no more. Hot water filled the mug and with a quick stir with the spoon, I was now ready to sit down and read the paper. Finally feeling a little more normal. I jumped up onto the stool, rested one hand against the breakfast bar and the other one tightly wrapped around the mug handle. I took a little slip of coffee and froze. My mind going into hyperdrive. As I stared down at the headline on the cover page of the paper in front of me…. BODY FOUND IN THE WEAR.

# CHAPTER 2
# THE BODY

Staring down at the headline BODY FOUND IN THE WEAR. All I could do was stare, frozen to the stool, like a shocked ice sculpture. The only thing that snapped me out of it and back to some reality was the glimpse of steam rising for my mug of hot coffee, that I caught in my peripheral vision and feeling the warmth emitting from it hit my cheek. But I still couldn't take my eyes off the front page. I finally raised my hand up and took a sip of my drink. With that I used my free hand to pull the paper closer and read on a little more. The sub text read *"There was a body found washed against the side of the riverbank near Fatfield bridge at 2:15am. The body is that of a male aged between 30 and 40 years old. Police have confirmed that the body has multiple wounds to the head and torso. The male in question has been identified as being that of Ben Stapleton, a local man from the Sunderland area. Police confirm that his body had only been in the water a short time. Police are asking for anyone with information in relation to the incident to come forward"*.

Seeing Ben's name written in text and knowing him personally, had my heart racing. Ben was in the same year as me at school. He was one of those popular kids in school, who everyone thought would become a footballer or equally amazing in anything he decided to do when leaving that hell hole. However, a bad injury to his knee and some even worse financial advice had put his life in a mess and he had to work from the ground up. I hated him at school, because all the guys wanted to be him and looking back, he was basically an arsehole. The opposite to me growing up. I was never popular at school and just did whatever needed to be done to pass those years away and leave with some qualifications. Since my school days and drinking in the same pub as him for years, I've changed my opinion of him for the better. He's not such an arsehole anymore and really is just a normal guy. We don't generally mix in the same social circles, but if he's in the bar we always make a small effort to catch up. Say "hi, how's things" stuff like that. It was quite nice to see him get back on his feet, secure job, wife and two kids (I think). Gill, the barmaid, always says that I look a little like him. I personally don't see it. Even some of my friends have mistaken me for Ben when we've been meeting up and he's standing at the bar. Similar size and hair I guess, our facial features are nothing like each other.

I think the one thing that had me in shock was that he left the bar last night about thirty minutes before me.

It could be Beth reading this paper with my name in it. All I can think about was what that would do to her and my sister. It was Connor that made me stay later. I owe him a pint next time I see him, or I could have been dead right now.

I drain my mug dry reading the sports section. Trying to take my mind of things between me and Beth and waiting for her to come home, so I can ask her opinion about going to the police. Not that I have much information, only that he was in the bar and left before me. The sports section was depressing me further. Sunderland had lost yesterday, and this was a reminder I didn't need. My hangover was subsiding slightly and now I'm starting to hit the tired mode. Even though I've only been awake for a couple of hours. I left the paper out on the breakfast bar to show Beth when she got home. I hopped off the stool and walked through into the living room. Turning on the tv and laying on the sofa, channel hopping through endless teleshopping crap to get to sky sports news. As I watched the chat and news snippets scroll along the bottom of the screen, my eye lids grew heavy. I started to fight it, but since Beth wasn't here, I thought a little sleep might do me good. I closed my eyes and the noise from the broadcasters became distant and in that moment I was out.

SLAM! Eyes shot open. At first, I didn't know where I was, eyes darting across a room I didn't recognise. My confused state between sleep and awake.

"Just me!" I was dragged back into the land of the living. That was Beth's house entrance, and the slam was her closing the door. The room I didn't recognise, was our living room. The same living room I fell asleep in. The same living room that I have sat in for years.

I glanced at my watch, 2:30pm. She'd been at her mams house for four hours. Nobody could cope with that woman for four minutes, let alone four hours. Beth usually goes around to see her once over the weekend, to check in on her and get her bit and bobs from the shops and things since losing her husband. I really liked Beth's Father. He was a great guy, who loved his family and loved his garden more. When we bought our house, it was her dad that helped me sort out the garden and gave me lot of tips to keep on top of it. Things like making sure to cut the lawn every two weeks and weed the borders whenever you have a spare five minutes, this keeps it looking good. His favourite saying, whenever he came to our house was "You could play bowls on that lawn kid".

I miss him a lot. We used to go to the social club on a Sunday afternoon to play cards and have a few beers. That was until his health deteriorated and he had a sudden and fatal heart attack. Now her mother is a different story. She is very interfering and rude at times. And since she'd lost her husband, she plays on it constantly, about needing jobs done around the house etc.

"Where have you been?" I ask.

"At my mams house." Beth replied, my turn to roll my eyes.

"How have you been there for four hours?" I ask, unable to believe it's possible to spend that much time with that woman.

"She gets lonely you know?" Beth isn't really paying attention to what I am saying and is busying herself plumping the cushions on the sofa.

"Yeah, but three hours yesterday and four today, I'm sure you're having an affair" I said, only half joking. "Shut up you and give me a kiss" She interrupts my speech. I couldn't keep up the moody persona after that and leaned in and gave her a kiss and a hug. Then she disappeared into the hallway.

"Have you eaten?" she shouted while taking off her hoody in the passageway and hanging it up on one of the hooks.

"No, but I could use some food" I yawn back to her, realising how hungry I am.

"Well get in here and help me then!" She laughs back at me.

When I entered the kitchen, Beth took one look at me. Hands on hips, head tilted to one side leaning against the kitchen worktop and said "Please, go and get dressed. I'm not eating my lunch with you dressed like a hobo".

I laughed, turned, and headed upstairs. I quickly put on some joggers and a t shirt and headed back to the kitchen. Where I was met with "Much better" I held my hands out in a gesture of "if you say so". While I was upstairs Beth had been busy. The oven was warming up and she had some pasta in one pan. Penne as I can't stand spaghetti, not that it tastes any different. I just don't like the mess and noise of eating it. And some lovely smelling tomato sauce in another. I assumed we are having pasta bake, if not she's heating the oven for no reason. I was correct.

"Pasta bake ok?" She asked, not that I had much of choice in the matter.

"Good for me" My tummy was grumbling now.

Once all the food items had been mixed together and poured into a baking dish, the ones with the high sides. Then some grated cheese on top. Shop bought grated, as I don't think we own a cheese grater. It went into the oven to melt and brown up. That should take a few minutes. Beth went over to the fridge and pulled out a bottle of white wine. Holding it up in front of me she said, "Are you brave enough to join me in a glass of this with dinner or are you being a moody, wuss all day?" laughing as she spoke.

My head was still a little fuzzy, but I agreed to join her with a glass of wine, as I thought we could unwind after lunch on the sofa. I got up and grabbed two (large) wine glasses from the cupboard behind me and set them on the breakfast bar in front of her. Beth proceeded to pour. Looking up at me with a face like 'tell me when to stop'. I waved my hand when it was half full and she poured the same amount into her glass.

Her phone chimed; she must have set an alarm for the pasta bake. I never do that; I rely on guess work mainly when it comes to cooking and she's a stickler for recipes and timings. She opened the oven door and the smell of melted cheese, and the heat from the dish wafted through the kitchen. She served up two pasta bowls full and left just enough in the baking dish for her dinner tomorrow. Re-heated pasta bake never tastes the same to me, but it's the ease of not having to prepare anything for her lunch the next day that she likes the most.

I lifted a heaped spoonful to my lips. "It will be boiling hot mind!" escaped her mouth. But it was too late. I burned my lips instantly.

"Fucking hell, you weren't kidding!" I gasped, mouth on fire. Beth just sat giggling.

I grabbed the glass of wine and took a big gulp, trying to extinguish the flames on my lips and roof of my mouth. I set the glass back onto the breakfast bar, gave one last huge blow from my mouth, like I was trying to blow out the candles on 70th birthday cake and said "Yeah, I think I'll leave that to cool down a little".

"Good idea honey" Beth soothed.

"Have you read the paper today?" I said, forgetting that she had been reading it this morning when I first made the dreaded, hungover decent of the stairs.

"Yeah, well I glanced through it really. why?" Beth replied, through half a mouthful of pasta.

"Did you read about the body being found? It was Ben. You know Ben, right?"

"Well, I don't really know him, just seen him around" she was well over halfway through her portion of pasta bake and my lips were still stinging from my own impatience.

"Well, he was at the pub last night and only left about half an hour before me" I commented nervously.

"OH GOD BABE, that could have been you!" she exclaimed in a shocked tone, and this was the first time that she had looked up from the bowl.

"I know love. I can't help thinking that if I walked my normal route and not over the green bridge, I might have found him, maybe even helped him. I felt almost guilty that I hadn't been there to help. For all the unintentional shit Ben caused me in my younger days, he didn't deserve to be robbed, murdered, and thrown in the river."

"How come you didn't walk your normal route, you know, the one that's actually lit up?" She said, with an almost, you never listen to me, and something/someone could have really hurt you kind of tone. I always get wrong off her for walking home.

"I don't honestly know love, I had a few too many". I replied apologetically.

I finally built up the courage to finish my pasta and Beth set the bowls and cutlery into the dishwash. Hands down the best thing I ever bought. We lay around on the sofa the rest of the day. My mind racing, about something that happened the night before. For the life of me I couldn't remember what. After her show had finished on TV, me watching too and I couldn't tell you a single thing that happened in it for the whole hour, she said she was off to bed. A quick glance at the time, it was 10:00pm maybe time for me to get some sleep too. After we climbed that wooden hill again for the final time today we jumped in bed, her in full PJ's as she's constantly cold and me nude, as I'm constantly warm.

"Good night honey" and she gave me a kiss on the lips. I returned "Good night, babe" with the lights off. I tried to sleep. Sleep didn't come. Maybe it was the fact that I slept on the sofa earlier for hours napping, but I think it was more to do with what I remembered about the night before.

"Are you still awake love?" I said while gently squeezing her upper thigh.

"No" was her response.

I laughed slightly and said, "I need to speak with the police tomorrow" and rolled over to sleep.

# CHAPTER 3
# SLEEPLESS

Waking up from thirty-minute intervals of sleep, sometimes cold after kicking off the bed covers, sometimes covered in a sheen of sweat from being buried under the covers like some kind of bed mole. Each time taking between twenty and thirty minutes to finally get back to sleep. My mind wouldn't switch off, the more I tried not to think at all, the more I went into deep thoughts, digging and digging a bigger and deeper hole of thought and sleep couldn't be found at the bottom, constantly out of reach.

*I was staggering slightly along the narrow gravel path of the riverbank, only wide enough to walk on. But that didn't stop the kids and sometimes adults tearing along it on their dirt bikes. Knowing fine well that the police wouldn't follow and even if they did, there were ample opportunities to escape the clutches of the law via one of the many small tracks leading to various housing estates. My route home was pitch black, lit only by the moon light shining down between the overarching trees.*

*The council should really do something about those, cut them back or something.*

*I rummaged through my jean pockets for my phone, hoping the light function would offer me some sight along this twisting path. Bringing my phone out of my tight pocket, I think it's time to accept that these jeans have seen their day and I need bigger ones. Or maybe I should take up Beth's offer of joining her at the gym to get back in shape. If truth be told, I hate gyms. They are always filled with guys who think they're Dwayne Johnson and take more pics of themselves in the mirror than physically working out. Then there's the women, wearing the tightest gym pants known to man. Not that I would be complaining about the view. But I would find it hard to train with these girls having everything on show and the macho men around. I held my phone in my right hand and clicked the side button, instantly realising it had died about two hours ago.*

*Remembering that I'd forgot to message Beth that I was leaving the pub. Not that I could of anyway, with this thing being dead. I put the useless, large black plastic object back into my pocket. With a lot less struggle than I had trying to retrieve it. It looks like my hangover tomorrow won't be the only thing I'll be getting wrong for. She hates me walking home anyway. But now without a "I'm leaving now, won't be long" message.*

*I continued twisting along the riverbank walkway. I could hear a mixture of the trees rustling and they were almost taking to me in muffled, distant voices telling me to stop, my mind was playing tricks on me. It was like something from a horror film, with the wind talking in the darkness. Going more inland in places and then a swing to the left and I escape the overcast tree limbs and see the water again. But something looked different. In my drunken haze I stopped to admire the river. Water rippling under the shimmer of light from the moon resting on it. Looking like the river is going to bed under its moon covers. It was beautiful. Thinking I need to get a picture of it for Beth. She has been looking for a picture for the living room of a local attraction and this could well be it. My phone struggle once more and the annoying realisation that it's still dead. I wonder how many more times I'll subconsciously forget about that on the way home. I guess she'll have to wait a little longer for the perfect picture.*

*While I was stood there, admiring the same view I've been admiring since I was old enough to explore these areas, I saw a parked car on the opposite riverbank. Roughly about a quarter of a mile to my left. It was a big car. Pretty flash motor. It looked black, but from this distance, with this light and my hazy, drunken eyes it could have been any colour. Its headlights were shining onto the water, from the parking area. I must have walked right past it, when I had lost the river, briefly under the cover of the trees and the dark wind voices.*

*It wasn't something unusual that a car would be parked there. It was quite a good spot for young lovers to park up away from prying eyes and have some fun. Me and Beth used to do it quite a lot, when we both still lived with our parents and the only opportunity to have our own space and a little freedom was when I passed my driving test and bought my first car. We would go for a drive to McDonalds, load up on food and take a drive down here. Eat our Big macs and then kiss for hours. Until I had to get her home before 11 o'clock. Naturally the kissing moved onto other things. The best night of my young life was when me and Beth moved onto heavy petting. The memory of that night will last forever, for two reasons. Firstly, it felt new and amazing. Secondly, just before we went full blown into it. A guy knocked on the window to ask if we'd seen his dog. Beth screamed and I nearly had a heart attack on the spot. I secretly think he just wanted a closer look and I make a joke of it now with Beth. She doesn't find it amusing, she isn't the same as she used to be. She was much more daring then.*

*I left the view behind me and continued my journey along the riverbank. I had to stop for a pee. I found a little spot behind some bushes and started to release the tension. I don't know why I felt the need to hide from sight. It was about twelve at night and absolutely no one around. Or so I thought. Mid way through my relief session I heard distant footsteps. Fast footsteps, not sprinting speed. Closer to jogging speed. But they continued to get louder and louder and were fast approaching my hidden spot. I was nowhere near finished behind the bushes, but no one could see me. The foliage was dense, and I could see out to the path, but unless whomever was approaching was specifically looking for me, they wouldn't know I was there. I decided to nip the end of my thing to stop any splashing sounds hitting off the leaves like you see and hear on any show that includes a rain forest. The footsteps were upon me, and I could clearly see the man's face. It was Bibby, the local down and out guy. He had been in the bar earlier asking for cigarettes, from everyone. Until he asked Chris that is. Who in the most heartfelt and as kind as Chris could be tone, told him "Fuck off, you little toss pot and find somewhere else". Him and Bibby have a little bit of history.*

*When the footsteps and passing smell of stale beer had passed by and off down the path I'd just walked, I stepped out from behind the bushes and put myself away. I had clearly forgot to shake properly as I could feel a tiny couple of damp spots on my inner thigh. No doubt they'll show up on my jeans, like I've just put two wet pound coins in my pocket. I set off again to home and bed.*

*So why was he running? The guy couldn't run a bath, never mind a run around the riverbank and why in that direction? He lived in the flats about ten minutes' walk further than my house.*

This needs to be told to the police. It's probably nothing. But if it's any use at all, then I'll gladly share it. A little more sleep came for me, and I woke up startled, as if waking from a nightmare where you're falling, and shudder awake just before you hit the bottom. But I couldn't remember falling in the dream. A quick glance at my phone 04:35. Thank God it's alive this time, I don't think I could cope with the disappointment. Placing my phone down and a roll over to reach out for Beth's thigh. Which again was missing, for the second day in row. Just empty bedding and feeling of nothingness. I could hear something from across the landing. It wasn't unexpected, as Beth often plays a podcast loudly while getting ready to go for her morning gym routine before work. The gym had certainly been working for her. She had lost a little weight and toned up her arms and bottom. Her bottom, being the best part. I didn't have a chance to get back to sleep, so I laid there for a little while, before jumping up and going for my usual naked walk across the landing to the bathroom.

"What are you doing up so early?" she said with a startled look, while turning off the podcast.

"Couldn't sleep very well and I remembered who I saw on the walk home on Saturday night" I said over my shoulder while taking the longest piss in history. "Even on the dark side of the river? You know, the one that's dangerous" she said, with a smirk across her face. "Disobeying your strict orders of safety, actually might have saved my life" I couldn't help my sarcastic tone as I smacked her on the bottom. She did a little startled jump.

"I know you're dashing out now, but how about we have an early night tonight and you could wear some saucy lingerie?" I asked with a raised eyebrow.

"Nothing would thrill me more than parading around the bedroom in those for you. But unfortunately, I'm working late and then I need to go and see my mam again" she said in reply but didn't really seem disappointed.

"Fucking hell Beth! We haven't had sex in weeks, if it's not your mam, it's fucking work or the gym!" I shouldn't have raised my voice like that, but I was angry in the moment. "I'm sorry for shouting" I apologised immediately.

"I'll make it up to you babe. On Sunday I promise. All day of me" she said that line and grabbed my crotch, with a little squeeze.

"Why Sunday and not Saturday?" I said with a quizzical look on my face.

"Well, I'm going on a spa day Saturday and drinks straight after with the girls. Plus, you have the boys coming round for a poker night, right? And I'm sure you don't want me parading around in that white lace set in front of your friends" her little wink was my cue to back down.

"Yeah, you're right, I guess". I had completely forgotten about the guys coming round on Saturday. It had supposed to have been the Saturday just gone, but Dylan couldn't make it at the last minute. So, we decided to go to the pub instead. Which was equally great. It'll be nice to catch up with Dylan on Saturday, I haven't seen him for a couple of months now. He hasn't been coming down the pub too often. I think he is a bit tight on cash at the minute and working overtime to pay for his wife's lifestyle. She lives a champagne lifestyle on lager wages. Not a good mix. Beth and Sarah don't get on well. They are constantly bickering or in competition. Whether it's hair styles, nails, figure, cars. You name it and they will be competing over who has the best. Beth always wins in the looks department. She is naturally pretty, with a great figure (even before the gym obsession) and personality to go with it. Sarah is just a fantastic plastic kind of girl. Bleached hair, fake tan and always wears clothes that are a bit revealing. Having said that, she has always been kind and nice to me. The one thing that Sarah has over Beth, is that she has kids. Me and Beth tried for children after we got married, but it never really worked out for us. We decided that we didn't want to go through the whole testing situation as we both didn't want it to feel like it was one person's fault. We just agreed to continue as we were and if pregnancy came knocking then we would welcome it.

Beth left the bathroom and headed downstairs. I went into the shower to freshen up and wash the lack of sleep from my eyes before I had to start getting ready. As I'm drying myself with the towel, an old towel. The ones that exfoliate you by accident.

Beth shouts up "See you later babe" and slams the front door (again). Sending a ripple through the house. As I walk into the bedroom, I open the blinds, looking down from the window, I see Beth's Mercedes running and her in the front seat, she's playing with her phone. Probably trying to select some music on Spotify. I had the sudden awareness that I was standing at my front bedroom window, completely naked. I rushed to the other side of the room to grab some boxer shorts to put on when I heard the car roar off the drive and into the distance.

I had meetings most of the day, so I decided on a white shirt, green tie, and navy pants. Accompanied by some nice brown leather brogues. I headed downstairs, picked up my laptop case and headed to the door. My phone vibrated before I reach the door handle. I put down my laptop case and fished the phone from my pocket (much easier in properly fitting trousers) as I had a message. It was from Connor.

"Have you heard about Ben?"

"Yeah, I read about it in the paper, terrible news" I quickly typed as I left the house and closed the door (not slamming it), all locked and headed to my car, placing my laptop bag on the back seat, amazed that I remembered to pick it back up from the hallway floor. My phone went off again as I got in the front seat

"Yes, it is terrible. You'll need to ring up and give evidence. I did it yesterday. Are you still wanting those recordings you were talking about on Saturday?"

"Yes, I'll ring them today and yes please mate" I replied without thinking.

"If you're sure, I could get them by Wednesday/Thursday" he replied, along with a quizzical looking emoji at the end.

"Thanks mate, I owe you one" and started up the engine. My phone went again, Connor wrote "No need to thank me, I hope you don't find anything".

"So do I my friend, but I must know the truth". And I throw my phone into the centre console and the second car left the house that morning.

# CHAPTER 4
# BACK TO WORK

The drive into work was a blur of traffic, brake lights and red lights at what seems like every junction. I was recounting the memories of my broken night's sleep, searching for more clarity around what I remember. Before I ring the police a little later and recount what information I have. There was nothing to find. With the amount of alcohol, I had consumed I was self-conscious about ringing them. Would they take the nights account of a drunken guy stumbling home? Would they just humour me and file my statement in B1N the moment I came off the phone? I had to tell them what I saw. If only for my own sanity. I needed to get the information out in the open and hopefully then, I might be able to relax and get some sleep, finally.

I pulled my car into the car park and headed to my designated "director parking" slot. I still haven't got used to the special treatment I now receive since getting my promotion. The way people now look at me differently and the jobs worths who crawl around hoping for work related handouts. You know the type, the people who call me "Boss" instead of my actual name. Unbeknown to them, that the moment I get the right opportunity they will be out of the door and replaced with normal, hardworking people. I've worked hard all my life to get to this position. All the way from sweeping the shop floor, while the other guys made the furniture. Taking every step on the ladder that was offered to me until I reached this position. I wasn't the most popular choice, amongst the other staff. Mainly because of my age. There were two of us vying for the position. Me, mid-thirties, up and comer and Billy Waites. Who had been at the company for as long as I've been alive. But if truth be told, he was the laziest person on earth. He was constantly getting others to do his work. Just because they see him as the senior person around here. When I got the job over him. He wasn't very happy and started some little hate group where the others would start to refuse to do things and start complaining about higher management failures. They didn't last long. Billy broke down in his disciplinary hearing, apologising for his behaviour and admitting that he had took my promotion over him to heart. I gave him a second chance. As he was close to retirement now anyway and it would actually save the company some money in the long haul by not having to settle him out of the business.

Now I'm finally comfortable at last. Both financially and work life balance. I could go for the regional managing director position at some point, but I don't like the idea of travelling up and down the country and living out of a suitcase, jumping from one hotel room to the next. If I was a single man, then maybe that life would appeal to me. But I'm a married man and would miss that too much, it wasn't worth the hassle, just for a few extra thousand in the bank.

It was now nearly 7:30am and I had planned to phone the police while I was still sat in my car. But the moment I switched off the engine, a couple of the "jobs worth" crew were lingering around. Waiting to walk into the office with me and ask the generic Monday morning questions. Like, "Hey Boss, good weekend?" and they always receive the same answer of "It was ok, quiet". Why don't they just ask the question that they really want to. "Hey Boss, if I keep asking you stupid shit question and make you coffee, can I have a raise?" at least then I might respect their honesty.

I walked into the main office and after a round of "good mornings" I headed to my separate office to get set up for the day. I was just opening my laptop when in walked Julie, with a cup of coffee especially for me. Julie was my personal assistant. She was about ten years older than me and more of a mother figure than a work colleague. As she set down my favourite cup, the one with He-Man printed on it. She said "Good morning, Boss" with a wink. She knows I hate it. "I see your little followers were making sure you got from your car to the office safe" with the added laughter. I had to smile at this point.

"I wish they'd fucking leave me alone!" the moment I said it with a raised voice, I instantly regretted it. It wasn't Julie's issue. "I'm sorry Julie, just had a rough night" I proclaimed in a soft tone that I knew would get her back on my side.

"Forget about them. Anyway, did you have a nice weekend?" she asked it with genuine curiosity "I had a night out on Saturday and regretted it most of Sunday" she laughed again at that.

"You men never know when to stop. Anyway, I'll leave you to it. If you need anything just let me know"

"Thanks Julie, you're the best".

"I know" and with her little cheeky wink and a swivel of her ample hips, she strode through the open door and closed it quietly. Maybe I should get Julie to give Beth some lessons on how to close doors properly.

I had an online meeting at 8:00am, so I thought I'd try a contact the police before I had to attend that. The phone only rang once, and the desk sergeant picked up immediately.

"Hello, you're through to Northumbria police. My name is DS Straughan. How may I be of assistance?" She had the most welcoming voice; at that point I could have told her anything she needed.

"Hi, thanks for picking up so quickly" I said in a quivering voice, suddenly remembering that I hadn't spoken to the law before in this scenario and didn't expect the first time to be in relation to a potential murder inquiry. I continued after a brief pause.

"I'm contacting you in relation to the news article I read about Ben Stapleton being found in the Wear. I had seen that it said, anyone with any information should come forward. I have some information I need to pass on. Do I tell you or someone else?" I was rambling through my words, feeling uneasy and almost nervous.

"Thank you for coming forward, sir. And you don't need to be worried about passing on any information" she could sense my tone of unease within a few seconds of our conversation.

"Thank you for being understanding, I just need to get it off my chest. So, do I tell you or someone else?"

"I will pass on your contact details to the Detective inspector who is dealing with the case, DI Morrison or another will contact you shortly" her voice was so calming, it put me at ease almost instantly.

"Do you need my details?" I was puzzled at how they would contact me without details.

"No sir, I have your details in front of me now. We will be in touch and thanks again for coming forward" "Thanks" and with that the phone was dead.

I made it on time to my morning meeting, not that I took anything in. My mind was a blur, and I was constantly talking through, what I would say to Mr Morrison in my mind. Sorry DI Morrison. Secretly praying that I would be articulate and concise in my account of what I saw. I was second guessing my route home. Was it Bibby I saw? Was it just someone that looked like him? No, no, no, it was him. I couldn't mistake his face. But would me seeing him and telling the police so, make a difference? Ben was an athletic guy, broad shoulders, and big hands. In my mind, there is no way that Bibby could take down Ben let alone rob him, kill him, and throw him in the river. Bibby was a scrawny, small guy. A couple of years younger than us and he could barely lift a cigarette paper. But what do I know, he could have caught Ben off guard and done God knows what terrible things to him before he finally hit the water. I had a sudden sense of guilt. Here I am, condemning a man (I use the term man loosely) to a life in prison for something that he may not have even done. Plus, he was on the opposite side of the riverbank with me. He could be telling the police right now that he saw me and that I could potentially be a suspect. Or maybe he saw something else and that's why he was running. Running away from something or someone. I'm over thinking everything at the moment and this meeting is still rolling on.

For all of Bibby's flaws the one thing that he does right in his life, is trying to take care of his mam and sister, who both live with him at the flats. I admire him for that. They had nothing growing up and that's why he is what he is. He has always stolen things, trying to sell knocked off goods down the pub. Mainly for his drug habits, but also to keep a roof over his family's head. He will never change; he didn't have a good start in life and for as long as I remember he has never had an official job. A few days here and a few days there, doing whatever. All cash in hand work. He did used to be a window cleaner for a little while. But Chris always says that was just a cover up to see what people had in their homes for him to steal at some point.

The meeting finally ended. I only realised it was over when the little faces on screen woke me from my daze and thoughts with a chorus of "Thanks, Bye, see you soon" and my face was the only one left on screen. I couldn't help staring at it for a while. I looked drained and exhausted. Heavy, lack of sleep bags under my eyes. A stubble that could do with a trim and freshen up. I looked about fifty years old this morning. What is happening to me? Too much drinking, not enough sleep, and the worry that my wife is having an affair, again have all took their toll on me, both, mentally and physically. And now the added worry that I'm expecting a call back from the local DI Morrison to recount my story.

I heard a faint knock on my office door, then I saw Julie's head pop around the edge of it.

"Can I come in?" she spoke with a certain calmness in her voice. The only voice I wanted to hear in this office was hers.

"Of course, you can. Come in and take a seat, I could do with some normal company for a while" after saying that in strode Julie, my one honest confidante in this whole place. I could tell her anything and she was never judgemental and never passed on any rumours. After taking her usual seat, she smiled and spoke.

"You look tired today, is everything ok at home, Boss?" adding the Boss part as an attempt to lighten the tone of her question.

"In honesty Julie, I think Beth might be cheating on me, or at least my mind is drawing me to that conclusion" I purposely left out the part, where I'm worrying about speaking to police and making a statement about the night when Bens life was no more.

"I'm sure she isn't, I've seen the way she looks at you, she loves you very much. Oh, and before I forget, Hannah wanted to speak to you, apparently Beth phoned her and asked her some questions about you last week." That came as I surprise to me. Why is my wife phoning my work, and especially HR Hannah, the biggest jobsworth of them all.

"What is Beth doing ringing her?"

"I assume it's the same thing she phoned her for last year, to put some holidays in for you and take you away for a few days for your birthday. It is next month after all" she has a way of calming my thought process.

"Yeah, that'll be it. Do you mind speaking to Hannah and confirming? I hate surprises". I really do.

"I know you do, that's why I've emailed her for the details already. You can do without a three-hour conversation about nothing in general with that woman." Julie rolled her eyes.

"You're the best Julie" I said with genuine sincerity.

"I know I am. You might have to wait a few days for the facts though. I got her out of office email earlier and she isn't back in until Friday. I'll leave you to it" and she stood up and strode out of my office for the second time today.

The rest of my day was a blur of meetings, reports, and endless cups of coffee. I still had no phone call back from DI Morrison. As I was packing up my things, putting my laptop away in my fancy Hugo Boss laptop case that Beth bought me as a present for getting my promotion, I felt my phone vibrate in my trouser pocket. I always have it on silent in the office and almost always forget to turn the sound up when I leave, leading me to constantly miss texts and phone calls after I drop my phone on the radiator cover at home, until I check the next morning. They are almost always stupid videos or memes from the group chat anyway. The vibration only lasted for a second which means it was a text. And my heartbeat could settle down. After (easily) retrieving my phone, the text was from Beth.

"Remember I'm going straight to mams tonight, so you'll need to sort out your own tea".

"Yeah, I remember" I quickly typed as I walked through the now half empty office and headed to my car.

I started the engine and for the first time today, I thought of something other than the call back I was waiting for. Food, I hadn't eaten today, and I was feeling it now. I could just go to McDonalds and relive my happy youth, when me and Beth used to think we were so grown up and free of our parents. But then I realised that if I did go for food at McDonalds, then I would be hungry again, about twenty minutes after eating and my waistline could do without the extra bulk. Then I remembered that my sister had text me last week, she never rings. It was about going around to hers and that she hadn't seen me in forever. That was another text that I missed, and I left it too long to reply and forgot to do that too. Claire was a great cook and I guess she would be home; some nice food and I get to catch up with her and my nephew for the evening. I quickly text her.

"Any chance I could come over now? sorry for the late reply".

"Yes of course" Was her reply, almost instantly, she was certainly at home. She was probably sitting on the sofa, scrolling Instagram or whatever other social media crap she was on. I headed away from the office on the ten-mile journey over to Claires.

I pulled up outside of her house. I have finally gotten used to calling it her house and not mams house.

Our father passed away when we were little and our mother passed away ten years ago and left the house to me and Claire. Claire was renting a house at that time with her then boyfriend, now husband, in a rough area. Not that this area is a shining light, but it's certainly better than where she was living. I already had a house with Beth, and we were settled, so I gifted my share of our family home to Claire and Alex so that they would be secure and didn't have to worry about rent payments. Alex is a good guy; a hard-working guy and he dotes on Claire and little James. He is a little older than me, by two years, which makes him close to seven years older than Claire. Little James is eight years old now. Thank god Beth sorts out the birthday cards and presents, that's the only reason I remember his age, because of the big number eight on the front of the card I had to write out a few months back.

I can still remember the day he was born. I don't think I will ever forget that experience. Alex was working away on the oil rigs, and I got a call early Sunday afternoon from Claire saying that she was in labour. She wasn't due for another month. With my mother now gone and Alex being five hours drive away and that was if the helicopter could get him off the rig right now, which I very much doubted. Claire asked if I could take her to the hospital, of course, I said yes straight away and as soon as I came off the phone, I begged Beth to come with me.

She refused, and said "She didn't ask me, she asked you. Now go and be a good big brother". I hopped in my car and headed straight over to her place. I had to help her down the stairs and into the car. The journey was a haze. A mixture of street signs, and pained moans from Claire all the way there. I was trying my hardest to console her, as she was terrified that something was going to be wrong with the baby, with him coming so much earlier than her due date. I pulled into the carpark as close to the entrance as possible, still about a hundred yards away. I ran over to the parking machine. I'm still angry about having to pay for parking while she was about to give birth. Any excuse for this country to squeeze as much cash out of people as possible. But that wasn't the worst part. After paying for the parking, I turned and saw Claire on her hands and knees on the tarmac between the painted white lines of a vacant space next to my car making some very strange noises. "What are you doing?" I said, as I raced back towards her. "He's coming now" she said through gritted teeth. "NO, NO, NO!" was my response. No way was my little nephew going to be born in the middle of a car park. I reached under her and helped her back to her feet. She couldn't walk and thankfully a woman entering the maternity building had heard us. She ran inside and within a minute, three other women in purple scrubs came running across the car park with a stretcher in the middle of them. They got her inside, and I expected the birth to be over in a matter of minutes. I sat by her bedside in a daze. Midwives and doctors coming and going, I heard sounds but couldn't make out any words. I was lost in my own world. When finally, I was brought back into the room when I heard the words "He's stuck". What seemed like seconds later, we were in a different room. This one more clinical. Almost surgical. I looked down and I was dressed in scrubs. I don't know how I got there, but I was holding Claires hand, and she kept thanking me, for what I don't know. I was of no help to her at this moment. I looked down over the blue separation screen. Dividing the top half of her body from her bottom half and then the cries and a little head appeared over the screen, held in a stranger's arms.

After she had been sewn back together and was able to hold him for the first time. She said "James, that's my hero right there" looking up at me. I burst into tears, as that was the first time, I had heard his name. She had named him after our dad. "I'm no hero, but you're my little sister and I love you. And now I love this little guy too" She smiled as she stared down at her little boy. I knew in that very moment that James would grow up having the best and most loving mother any little boy could wish for.

She and James slept for a good few hours, as I held her hand and then the door swung open and there was

Alex, still dirty from work and obviously tired himself. He must have left as soon as he could from the rig. He placed a hand on my shoulder and looked at them sleeping. "Was everything ok?" were the first words he spoke. I stood up and presented him my chair, he looked like he needed it. "I'll let Claire fill you in when she wakes up. Enjoy them Alex" I said as I left the room. I sat in my car in the carpark and cried for over an hour. It was the most traumatic and wonderful experience of my life. That feeling will have been ten times greater for Claire.

I turned off the car's engine and as I got out and closed the car door, Claires front door opened and out ran James. I walked to the gate and was greeted with a huge hug from him. One of those hugs where he jumps at me and I must catch him in mid-air, spinning him around. He was squeezing me so tight. The only thing I could think of, was that I need to make more of an effort with this little guy. He is so much fun, and it can't be easy on him with his dad working away for weeks on end. As I finally started to lower him to the ground and the spinning had stopped. I was now back facing the front door, and slightly dizzy. Claire was now standing at the front door; with the most welcoming smile I have ever seen.

"He looks like he's missed his fun Uncle. Come on you two dinners got about thirty minutes left".

I couldn't tell if the smile was for me or that she was happy that her little boy was happy to see me. Either way, it felt warming to me, and I knew that I was going to be looked after, if only for a few hours.

"Thirty minutes until tea?" I ask with a wry smile.

"Yeah" Was her quick response while turning to head back into the house (her house now).

"Well, if we have thirty minutes, would you mind if I take James for a walk to park?" I said, while looking at James with raised eyebrows.

"Yes please, mam is that ok?" In his little delighted tone. "Ok, ok, but only for half an hour, you got that? And that warning goes to both of you" Claire responded with that smile again and closed the front door.

Me and James had a little high five and then he grabbed my hand and we set off, across the road.

# CHAPTER 5
# ROUND AND ROUND WE GO

We made the little adventure around the corner and across the street to the park. But when we got there the steel gates were closed and padlocked. I did what every guy does in that situation and gave the padlock a pull, never in the history of mankind has any padlock, miraculously opened by doing that. This lock was no different. It stayed locked, exactly as it was intended to, another success story for the padlock inventors. I turned around and saw James's expression change. His cute little smile had faded into a solemn and joyless expression. Like if someone had just stolen his favourite toy and wouldn't return it. He looked up at me, I could see that he was expecting me to say something like "Sorry James but it looks like we'll have to get you home" but I couldn't do that to him. Instead of saying anything I just picked him up with a hand under each arm and carefully lowered him onto the other side of the steel bars. Thank God that the gates were only up to my waist. His face turned to joy once more as I said "Shhh, your mam can never know".

"Our secret" was his response while mimicking him zipping up his mouth with his little hand. I hadn't really thought this through properly. As I now had to get on the other side of our metal blockade. While James straightened up his t-shirt, which had ridden up his chest from me lifting him over. I placed both hands on the top of the cold metal railings. I took a deep breath, filling my lungs and with one big push of my arms, I vaulted into the air and both of my leather shoe clad feet came landing down onto the soft, freshly cut grass. I was astounded that I hadn't fallen. Maybe I'm not too much out of shape after all.

After I composed myself, I looked up and James was already running over to the roundabout, kicking up cut grass in his wake. He leaped onto it, and it instantly started spinning.

"Come on, I bet we can make it go really fast" he shouted across the playpark at me, in his own little enthusiastic way. I walked over and put one foot on the roundabout, and it brought back memories of me and Dylan playing on this park together when we were kids. Remembering how fast we used to make this thing go around, and clinging on for dear life, thinking that if we let go, we could shoot straight up to the moon. Dylan is my oldest friend. We have known each other since we were about four years old. We grew up in the same street and went all the way through school together. It's such a shame that he ended up with that bitch, and we don't see nearly enough of each other anymore. Maybe he says the same thing about Beth.

My foot now planted on the roundabout and my other foot scooting the ground to build up some speed.

"You better hold on tight little buddy" I could listen to his laughter all day. His knuckles grew whiter as his grip on the bars grew tighter, the faster we went.

"Woohoo" as I planted my second foot onto the roundabout. We faced each other and I tried to concentrate on him and not the repeated background objects that passed through my vision every second with each rotation. I knew I would be dizzy from this, but I didn't care. I felt like that little boy again, who had no cares in the world, only living to have fun with his best friend. The roundabout gradually began to slow down, those blurred background objects, becoming more visible with each passing. As the roundabout was almost at a stop. James and I jumped off at the same time, then my legs started to wobble. James was stumbling on his little legs, trying to walk forward, but ultimately going backward. I went off to the side like a crab and grabbed hold of a 'no dogs allowed' sign, just in time to see James fall and land on his bum in fits of laughter.

As my legs finally settled and my vision returned to its normal self, I could see James had risen back to his feet and was currently using his hands to brush the cut grass from his bum and legs. I could see over the top of James head, a black range rover driving up the street. Not too fast, but fast enough to hear the engine roar. The car pulled up outside of Frankie's house. Frankie was the local drug dealer, he dealt in nothing too heavy, just weed and the odd time cocaine. It was like a family business, my uncles used to buy their weed from Frankie's dad, at that very same house. He was also called Frankie. Very original I know. The passenger side door opened and out stepped a very smartly dressed guy, black suit, and brown shoes. The guy was massive, I could see his suit stretching to cover his huge frame from a hundred yards away. They must be undercover cops, paying Frankie a visit, to check in on him and make sure he hasn't gone too far. I watched the guy walking up the front steps to Frankie's front door, but he didn't knock on it. Instead, he turned to his left and gently tapped on the living room window. Then he turned to face me. From this distance, I couldn't tell if he was looking directly at me or not, but I wasn't going to take any chances. I glanced down at my feet, to avoid any direct eye contact, not that I was even sure he was looking at me. Then my eyes went back to James, who was now heading towards the swings. I followed in his footsteps, pushing my feet through the cut grass, never raising my gaze above my shoes until I reached the swings, which James was already sitting on. I finally lifted my head to check if the guy was still looking, but all I saw was the front door closing, I had to assume that he went inside, as the Range Rover was still there, and the big guy was nowhere to be seen.

I was still a little out of breath from our whirlwind experience on the roundabout when I got over James, who was perched on one of the two swings.

"You can go on that one" he said, excitedly pointing to the free, swinging seat next to him.

"If I go on that one, who is going to push you so high that you'll touch the sky?" I responded with a wink.

He just laughed at that. As I walked around the back of James and give him a little push

"Is that high enough?" I said jokingly,

"Come on, put your back into it" laughing as he said it. "Ok, ok!" and with that I gripped the swing seat and drew it back, almost up to my head height and held it there. Holding him in suspense of when I would let him go. I let go just a little and caught it again, just like when you pretend to throw a ball for a dog and he jets off after it, while it's still firmly in your grasp. My arms began to ache and with that I let him go, he flew down through the air, feet almost hitting the ground and then he started his ascent into the sky. The joyous laughter and giggles as his view changed from grass to sky and back to grass was infectious. Another push and he was off again, even higher this time. I let him swing for a little while. Telling him to draw his legs in when going backwards and stretch them out when going forwards. I guess these lessons were Alex's job and he misses a lot, with working away. But James can tell him all about it at the weekend when he's home.

I sat on the free swing seat next to James as he kept going up and down. I was looking over at the Range Rover when Frankie's front door opened. Out walked the big guy and following behind him was Bibby. I guess that's where Bibby went that night. No the wonder he was heading in the opposite direction from home that night. When I saw him on the riverbank path he had his head hung low and his hand closed together in front of him. I couldn't see any handcuffs, but then again, my eyes weren't that good these days and I was a hundred yards away. But he still had that tracksuit on that he wore on Saturday night. So, I assume that he was hiding out at Frankie's. It maybe wasn't the best idea to lay low after committing a murder at a very well-known drug dealer's house. A house that Claire often tells me it gets raided by the police, every few weeks. As they slowly walked down the steps towards the parked car, the driver side door opened. Out stepped a tall man, also smartly dressed. This time in a navy tailored suit. He stepped around the car and opened the backdoor. He raised his hand up in a waving gesture back up to the house. That's when I saw Frankie standing there, in a pair of sports shorts, no shirt and covered in what looked like millions of tattoos, none of which looked professional done. The big guy proceeded to push Bibby's head down and landed him into the back seat. The tall man closed the door and they both got back into the front seats. Then the engine roared once more, and they took off down the street. Frankie was still standing at the door, he looked over and waved at me, I gave a courtesy wave back. We knew each other's names, just purely because we lived around the corner from each other for so many years growing up, but we have never been friends, or mixed in the same social pool. Frankie stepped back wards into his house and the door was closed.

James had finally come to a standstill on the swing. His hair was standing straight up from the speed of his fun going through the air. I laughed to myself about his hair, while glancing down at my watch.

"Look kidder, it's been almost twenty-five minutes since we left your mam, maybe it's time to start heading back. You're cute, so you'll be ok if we're late. But your mam will kill me" I said.

"Yeah, you're right... I am cute" it was his time to wink. I couldn't hold my laugh in, he is one hundred percent his mother's son.

"Do you come to the park often?" I asked the question, but I already knew the answer.

"Not really, Mams busy and Dads tired when he gets home for the weekend" He responded with a nature of maturity for someone so young. He knew that his Mam and Dad were working for him and a better quality of life for all of them.

"I'll make a deal with you, if we can leave now (to stop Claire from killing me) and go and have some great food that your Mam has been cooking, I'll come over every Monday night and we can go to the park or even the cinema sometimes if you like?" he didn't respond with words.

He just jumped off the swing, grabbed hold of my hand and started to pull me up from the swing seat. That was as good as any handshake deal sealer. We headed once more to the metal blockade. The same scenario in reverse this time, of me lifting him over the steel bars and my best attempt at hoping the rails and trying to look cool, while doing it, it was another success. We approached the roadside and James said "You have to look both ways" He must have been learning about the Green cross code in school. Nothing was coming so we crossed the road and headed back to Claires.

As James ran up the front steps to the front door. I could see Claire standing in the front window. Had I been too long at the park? I glanced down at my watch and realised that we were late, but only by a couple of minutes. Claire had disappeared from the window now and was now standing holding open the front door.

"Look at the state of you, you're covered in grass. But you're still a little cutie" she said with a wide grin.

I looked over to James and winked, we both remembered what I told him earlier, about his mam not getting mad at him for being late.

"Come on, dinner is sorted and on the table". Walking through the hallway, I noticed that Claire still had a picture of mine and Beth's wedding day. I looked so happy and proud, that I managed to marry the woman I love in that picture. The front door closed behind me, startling me out of my momentary daze.

"You're late Mr" Claire said with a finger pointing at me, which was exactly like my mother used to do, standing in the same spot only twenty years ago.

"I know, sorry" she smiled at that.

We all sat down at the table and Claire produced the biggest plate of food I've seen in a long time. Setting it down in front me, it smelled so good. I just stared at the huge steak, cooked to perfection. Well done, still juicy. But with no pink bits in sight. It was accompanied with roast vegetables and peppercorn sauce. I hadn't realised just how hungry I was, I couldn't wait to get stuck in. When I stopped staring at my food and looked up, Claire had her plate in front of her, the same food as me, but a slightly smaller steak. James had chicken nuggets and chips, with a large dollop of tomato ketchup on the side. "Come on eat up" No sooner had the words left her mouth, I had cut a large chuck of steak and raised it to my mouth. God, it tasted good. We all sat in relative silence until all our plates went from full to empty. Claire got up and said "Good?" while looking at me with eyes that seek approval. Both me, and James said at the same time "Perfect". Claire smiled and collected the plates and started washing them in the sink. I couldn't remember the last time I washed a dish in the sink, for the last five years we'd had a dishwasher. Claire spoke over her shoulder "Come on James, you need to go and take a shower and put your PJ's on, go on upstairs" James left the table and walked past me heading to stairs, not before giving me a high five on route.

While James was heading upstairs. Claire said "Where's Beth? I haven't spoke to her in ages".

"Oh, she's always around her Mothers or the gym. Or work, I can't keep up. She was at her Mams all day yesterday and she's staying over at hers tonight" I said, trying not to sound like a man who suspects his wife of having an affair.

"She was at her Mams yesterday? I told you I hadn't spoken to her in ages, but I saw her walking into Costa yesterday afternoon. I was driving by as I was taking Alex to the train station. Her Mother wasn't with her" she said, for the first time turning around from the sink to face me.

"She was probably waiting in the car" I said in a defensive tone. Claires voice rose as she said "Hey, did you hear about Ben?" quickly moving the conversation on to something else. Which I was very glad of.

"Yes, I did, I'm actually waiting for a call back from the Police about giving a statement" I was glad to move away from any chat about Beth, but this bombshell will have Claires attention for sure.

"Statement? Did you see who did it? You'll have been at the pub then?" the last part was a sly dig at my drinking habits.

"Yes, I was at the pub, but on my walk home I saw Bibby heading in the wrong direction".

"And you think it was him?" came back in her inquisitive tone. "I don't know what to think really, just that he was there, and Ben was found dead, oh and I actually just seen him get took away by two plain clothed policemen from Frankie's house" I forgot the last part even occurred until we started talking about the whole situation.

"Wow. Certainly, looks guilty then" That was Claire knocking the last nail into Bibby's coffin.

"Are you sure it was him? I mean, are you sure it wasn't just someone that looks like him, that you saw?" She was on a roll now, and I was feeding the gossip dragon.

"I'm sure, no one could miss that scar on his cheek".

"I still can't believe Chris did that to him" Claire said.

"I can, Bibby got Chris's little sister Kim out of her head on, god knows what drugs and was feeling her up while she was passed out. It's just lucky that it was in her house and Chris came home early, or who knows what Bibby might have done" I said in a tone that Claire understood, that if the tale was about her and not Chris's little sister Kim, I would have done exactly the same.

"Yeah, but did he have to smash his face through the glass coffee table?"

"Bibby jumped up and ran at Chris, Chris pushed him, and he fell through the coffee table, I've known Chris for twenty oh so years and he's not a malicious guy, he told me what happened that night" I think she believes me. I wasn't about to tell Claire the real story. That Bibby got his scare after Chris repeatedly kicked and punched him all over the house. When Bibby tried to get out of the front door, Chris grabbed him by his hair pulled him across the floor and smashed his face through the coffee table. Chris came around to my Mams house (Claire's house now) and I burned his clothes in the back garden just in case the police came looking for him, which they never did. I guess Bibby understood that if he grassed on Chris, it would open a whole investigation and Bibby would come off worse in the long run.

"So, one thing I could never get my head around. Why do you guys call him Bibby? His name is Paul Robertson, it has no connection to Bibby whatsoever" She asked the question that I'm quite embarrassed to know the answer to.

"Ok, so the Bibby name came around, because of the sheer volume of drugs he uses. He has lost most of his teeth through drugs and drools quite a bit, especially when he speaks. So, Dylan started calling him Bibby because he should be wearing a bib. But that was like twenty years ago and the name just stuck, now everyone calls him that. Even Bibby uses it, or certainly used to, you've seen his spray paint moniker on the walls at the back of the shops".

She burst into fits of laughter at this "I love the background to that name" she managed to blurt out between giggles. I looked down at my watch, it was close to 8:00pm.

"I better get going soon" I said with a voice that indicated that I didn't want to leave.

"Oh no, why do you have to go?" Claire said this with genuine upset in her voice.

"I'm sorry, but I need to get home and do some work, ready for tomorrow" Claire could tell by my tone how unhappy I was to go.

"Ok, will you shout up and say goodbye to James on your way out and don't be a stranger" she said, wagging her Mam finger at me again.

"I won't, I made a deal with James that I'll come round every Monday night to see him and you of course" I added a sarcastic tone to the last part.

"Oh, that will be great, we love having you here, and James will be talking about his park adventures for the rest of the week. Maybe you can bring Beth over too?" Claire said expectantly.

I thought about the Beth part and the main reason that she doesn't really come over here is because of little James. Not that she dislikes him or anything, the kid is as bright as a button and so much fun. It's because seeing James, only reminds her of what we can't have in our lives, a complete family.

"Maybe, let's see if she's busy with her Mother" that was the only response I could muster.

I know Claire understood the underline of why Beth hadn't been over in so long, but she never pressed it with me as an issue.

I gave Claire a big hug "Thanks for my tea sis, it was as perfect as always".

"Flattery will get you nowhere" She laughed in response.

As she gave me one last big squeeze and we were separated, I headed back down the hallway and opened the front door. I turn to look up the stairs and James was standing on the top tread, in his Star Wars onesie looking down at me.

"I got to go now kidder, but I'll be back next week for another adventure" He didn't respond with words, but I did get a double thumbs up from him and a huge grin. I closed the door and headed to my car. I checked my phone and I'd missed a text from Connor, I must try and remember to take my phone off silent. The text read "Your coat is still at mine" I replied "Bring it over with you on Saturday for the poker night" I got a thumbs up emoji as a reply.

# CHAPTER 6
# BEFORE THE NIGHT OUT

I stood under the shower, letting the warm water run over my head. Staring down at my growing belly and just seeing my toes poking out from under it. As I stood there in a world of my own, my mind led me to think about starting to go running again. I used to enjoy running, running along the river track in a big loop, involving crossing two bridges on route back home. It was only around three miles, but it was good. Having my headphones in, listening to AC/DC, mainly to drown out the sound of my laboured breathing and heavy foot fall on the dirt track. I must start doing it again, and maybe I could start to see more of my feet by doing so. I'm sure Beth would approve of me losing a few pounds and getting into shape. She was constantly trying to get me signed up at the gym and this would be a happy compromise for both of us.

The water pressure had become noticeably slower and that could mean only one thing, Beth was now in the bathroom using the wash basin. I turned around and there she was, washing her make up off. She was dressed for a night in, wearing bright patterned PJ bottoms, the ones with pictures of watermelons on them. On the top half of her body, she had a huge, oversized flurry hoody in dark grey. Looking like a woman who had been married for years and the need for dressing seductively for bed had faded from inappropriate to comfy attire. "Could you not have waited for me to finish in here?" I said, while peering around the shower screen.

"You have been in there for twenty minutes, and you say I take ages in the shower" was her response, in between splashing cupped hands full of water against her face, washing off the makeup removal cream.

"You could join me in here?" I was testing the water in the hope that she would jump in.

"You don't have time for that, you need to be at Connors in twenty minutes, for your boy's night" emphasizing the "Boys" part. I couldn't see her eyes rolling, but I know her, and she will have rolled her eyes at the last part. I didn't say anything in return. I just turned off the shower tap and reached around the shower screen for the towel blindly as my eyes were full of water. After I gave my face a quick wipe with the towel and now able to re-open my eyes. I noticed that Beth had gone, and I could hear her last steps on the bottom of the stairs.

We used to be so close, every Friday or Saturday was like a date night. Either going to the cinema, out for a meal or just going crazy and getting drunk in some nightclub. But ultimately late nights at the office from me and her recent obsession with the gym have put an end to those things. We still go out sometimes, but the conversation isn't the same. We used to be able to talk about absolutely anything. Now it's centred around work, some new girl at the gym or her Mother. I blame myself a little for her affair. Maybe if I had concentrated on her more, then she wouldn't have needed the attention from him. I guess that's the price I must pay for my dedication to work and landing a successful job.

After towel drying the rest of me, I had to get dressed and get out of the front door. I quickly ran from the bathroom across the landing to the bedroom naked, I am forever forgetting to close the landing blinds and I don't think the neighbours would appreciate seeing my white bottom on an early Saturday evening. I reached the safety of the bedroom in a few seconds, quickly put on some underwear and my socks and jeans followed straight after and my brand-new white trainers, fresh out of the box. I stood glancing into my wardrobe at the various tops and shirts, all a similar colour and I couldn't decide which one to wear. Trying to remember what I wore the last time I was out with the guys, so that I didn't wear the same thing two nights out on the bounce. I finally settled on a dark grey Hugo Boss jumper, not a thick one as I want to wear a coat tonight.

I made the journey down the stairs and popped my head around the living room door and saw Beth curled up on the sofa with a glass of white wine in her right hand and the TV remote in her left. It was no use asking her to drop me off at Connors, as she looks settled. She turned her head towards me.

"You look nice" she said, looking me up and down.

"Thanks, I'm going now" with that I leaned in and gave her a peck on the cheek as she had a mouth full of some chocolate bar, looking a little like some kind of wino hamster.

As I left the room, I heard her mumbling something. As I turned around, I saw Beth gesturing with her arms in some attempt to put her imaginary coat on. It was her cue for me to remember my coat. I lifted my hand and gave her thumbs up. I walked out of the living room, grabbed my wax jacket off the hook and struggling to put in on as I left the house and closed the door with my arm only in one sleeve in the jacket and finally getting the other one on as I reached the end of the drive.

Connor didn't live far away. It was only about ten minutes' walk, and the weather wasn't that cold, not like yesterday when it rained constantly. That's probably why I feel so tired, I didn't get much sleep last night as the rain was lashing against the windowpane in the bedroom and Beth's little snoring noises didn't help. Sometimes I think she sounds sweet and other times I could kick her during the night. As I crossed the road and stood on the loose paving, it rocked, I slipped just a little and when the paving settled it sprayed up muddy brown water across my trainers and some went high enough to land on my coat. Thankfully none landed on my jeans.

I instantly span around to see if anyone had seen me, as the embarrassment hit me like a shock wave. Just like when my mother found my porn magazines stuffed under my mattress. A stupid place to hide them when I think about it. Considering she was the one who used to change my bedding and sheets, and always flipped my mattress. I found the coast was clear of any sniggering passers-by that might have just witnessed the event, my thoughts went to my new trainers and that Beth would kill me for ruining another pair.

I was halfway between home and Connors when my unfortunate accident happened. Should I go home and change or just continue onto Connors? I decided on the latter. Purely because I couldn't be bothered with a mini argument about my trainers with Beth and it would have put me in a bad mood for my night out, the fallout can wait until the morning. It just means I'll have a hangover and a moody wife. I continued my route to Connors, reaching the corner of his street. He wasn't expecting me for another thirty minutes. But I needed to speak to him without Chris being there. I didn't want my situation becoming public knowledge and if Chris hears about it, he'll pass it onto Dylan and then Dylan would pass it on to his wife Sarah. Then she would take great pleasure in lording it over Beth at any event or barbeque that we attend as a couple in the future, and I can't have Beth finding out. Connor was a good guy he wouldn't blab about anything I told him in confidence.

As I approached his house, Connors next door neighbour was walking by.

"You been in the wars?" Was his passing comment.

I glanced down at my jacket and the mud splats had started to dry on the front.

"An unfortunate tripping hazard" I said with an embarrassed tone to my voice.

He just nodded, with a smile and continued to walk by, which I was glad about, as I could feel the blood rushing to my cheeks. I walked up Connor's drive and knocked on the door, as I waited a few minutes, I knocked again, whispering under my breath "For fuck's sake, answer the door" as I heard a rush of steps coming down the stairs and the door flew open. As Connor stood there with wet hair and towel covering his lower half from the rest of the street

"What the fuck happened to you?!" as he burst into a fit of laughter, leaning back with an outstretched finger pointing towards my flaws.

"I just need to clean up and then I'll be back to my best" Trying not to fuel his joking fire.

As a show to him that I wasn't embarrassed I turned to look at his car on the drive and commented

"I didn't know you were allowed to bring them home with you" I moved the conversation away from my appearance and to his bright white Volvo with the yellow and blue reflective markings and the blue light diffuser on the roof. It had Police emblazed across the side and over the bonnet.

"You can when you're one of the top boys on the force" Was his come back with a tap on my shoulder.

Connor had been in the Police force for as long as I could remember. He always wanted to join up, even when we were at school. Although, at the school we went to he got bullied and beaten up a few times because of his aspirations. Not that it stopped him from following his dream. I guess going through that at school, only made him more determined and I know that he has put a few of those bad lads behind bars over the years, either for drug related issues or driving offences. Connor lived the single life and never settled down to marry anyone. He had a string of girlfriends, but when they got too serious the relationships always ended. He was a career police officer and girls got in the way. Those were his words, whenever Chris would dig into his affairs, normally calling him a puff or something along those lines. He just brushed off the insults and carried on as normal. It was his police connections that I need to chat to him about.

I turn back toward the house and walked through his front door.

"You're early, aren't you?" as he looked up to the clock that hung from the hallway wall.

"Yeah, I need to ask a favour and I don't want anyone to know about it" I spoke while staring down at my mud splatted trainers.

"Sure, no problem, as long as it's not a sexual favour, we're good" with a slight chuckle emitting from his lips

"I need to get ready, go and get yourself cleaned up in the kitchen and grab a couple of beers, I'll be back down in five minutes and then we can talk".

With that he began running up the stairs, holding onto the towel as it began to slip down from his hips, and I headed into the kitchen. I took my coat off and threw it onto the back of a dining chair. That's when I saw the full extent of the splatters. My back was covered, how the fuck did it get on the front and back? I was looking out of the window into Connor's back garden, and I noticed that the clouds had parted, and it was sunny. I thought I might just leave my coat here. The walk home might be a bit chilly, but I'll have my beer coat on by then and won't feel it. I flicked off my trainers and grabbed some kitchen roll off the windowsill. I attempted to wipe the mud off, some came off but not a lot. I didn't dare use any water, as I didn't fancy walking around for the night in wet footwear.

As I was putting my trainers back on, Connor appeared at the door.

"Best I can do with these" looking down at my feet.

"No one will even notice. Now grab some beer. It looks nice outside; do you want to sit and enjoy a cold one in the sun?" It was a question that didn't need an answer, as Connor had already opened the patio doors and was starting to grab a couple of garden chairs and proceeded to dust them off with his hands before setting them down on the sun lit decking. I headed over to the fridge to grab the beer. You can tell Connor is single. The contents of his fridge consisted of milk, some cheese, a half an onion, a couple of cans of Coke and a full shelf of beer. I grabbed a couple, closed the fridge door, and headed out into the garden.

"Jesus Connor, I need to take you food shopping" I said as I passed him a cold can of beer. He just rolled his eyes (that's two people that have done that to me today) while I could hear the hiss and snap of the ring pull.

As we sat there for a few minutes, each taking a big gulp of cold beer. Feeling it slide down my throat and enjoying the sun beaming down across my face. Connor finally broke the silence when he placed his beer on the decking, I imagine he never intends to buy a garden table to go with these chairs.

"So, what's this secret favour shit all about?" Spoken like a true professional of the law.

For all my mouth was wet from the beer, it has never felt so dry, as I tried to find the words to ask. I could feel my tongue sticking to the roof of my mouth and a light sheen of sweat forming on my brow and it wasn't caused by the sun. This moment only lasted for thirty seconds or so and I raised the can once more to my parched lips, taking another big gulp. Trying to buy me more time to get the words right in my head and Connor had grown impatient.

"Come on man, blurt it out. You know you can ask anything right?" it was a rhetorical question. He knows that I already knew that of him. And the last part of his sentence put my worries at ease. After all Connor was the only person who knew about Beth's previous sexual indiscretions outside of wed lock. So, this shouldn't be too hard to ask after all.

I set down my beer, meeting Connor's on the decking and raised my eyebrows in a show to Connor that I'm getting to it at some point, just after I swallow my mouthful of beer.

"Ok here goes. Well, you remember what Beth got up to a few years back, right? With that guy from her work?" A simple nod from Connor was all I needed to allow me to continue.

"Well, I think she maybe up to her old tricks again" I paused.

"With the same guy?" Connor wondered.

"Now that, I don't know. I don't even know if she is having an affair at this point. It's just that she's spending a lot of time at her Mothers apparently and the gym" I was being open and honest with Connor and to be fair to the guy, he was taking it all in and trying to think about it logically. Basically, the opposite of me.

"So, you're basing this on what? A hunch? From what I can see, she is just going about her life and so should you be. Thinking like this, can't be good for you mate" his calming tone and reasoning response was what I had expected.

"It's not just those things, it's the sudden ending of phone calls when I get home or her phone vibrating through the night and me waking up to find her either replying to them or going to the bathroom with her phone. Which she only started doing a couple of months ago" after I finished speaking, I paused again. I could see from Connors face that he was trying to think of a supportive answer for me, but he couldn't.

All he could say was "I'm sorry man, that's got to be hard to live with" as he reached down, picked up both beers. He passed me mine and we both took a big drink.

"I don't know how I can help you, it's not like I can follow her, my car isn't the most inconspicuous is it?"

I smiled at that, but he didn't. I could see in his eyes that he wanted to help me, but he just didn't know how.

I broke the silence.

"Can you remember you telling me about that guy you caught, the one who was selling the cocaine to kids?"

"Yeah, I remember. I didn't catch him though, my partner did, through his phone records" When Connor finished speaking, I could tell by the way his head dropped ever so slightly to the side, that he knew where this was going. He didn't speak, I guess he wanted me to ask him directly.

"Ok the guy your partner caught then?" correcting my earlier mishap. Connor shifted in his chair. I could see that this was making him uncomfortable.

"So, the favour I need is for Beth's phone records. More specifically recordings of them" No sooner had the words left my mouth, Connor interrupted me.

"If and it's a big if I can do that, would it really help to know? If she is having an affair, do you really want to hear all of her sordid business coming from her lips?" The words he spoke were true. If I heard that it would crush me and then my life would be broken apart. A failed marriage and I probably couldn't afford to keep the house on my salary alone.

"Look Connor, I just need to hear the truth. I'm probably completely wrong and hope to God that I am. But I can't go on like this. It's killing me inside" as the last words escaped my mouth, I could feel that welling of tears, collecting at the bottom of my eyes, desperately trying to escape down my cheeks in a stream of sorrowful release. Connor could see that I was upset, he brough his hand down against mine, that was resting across my knee.

I still wake up in the middle of the night sometimes, to the sight of Beth and him together. The image will stay with me for the rest of my life. I had hoped on some level that it would pass in time, but that time never came. It was her own stupidity how I found out about it. She was very secretive about her work friends. Then after a summer party her boss held at his house. She started to dress differently for work. More tight-fitting outfits and wearing even more make up. Then after a couple of weeks. I started getting the odd text saying things like "such and such is leaving the company, and we are going out for drinks after work" and "I really need to get this report done so I'm staying back". Now none of those would be deemed as suspicious if it was a regular thing. But this was the first time she had ever done this and mixed with the outfit changes. Something didn't seem right. This went on for a couple of weeks and then one night my car had broken down and I had to be towed to the garage on the other side of town, next to Beth's office. After dealing with the oil clad mechanic and leaving the car there. I decided to walk across to her office, which was only a short five-minute leg stretch away. She was working late again, and the carpark was empty except for hers and another parked side by side at the edge of the carpark and away from the main building. That's when I caught her riding on some guy's dick in the passage seat of her car. She saw me and screamed, while jumping off his lap. It was the look on his face that still wakes me through the night, he had a huge grin while staring at me.

I couldn't do anything but walk away. I stayed out that night at a cheap hotel in the city centre and confronted her about it the next day. I hated her in the moment, but I did still love her. She left her job there and started a new one. We tried to move on from it. It took me a few weeks before I could even look her in the eye. Then another few weeks before I spoke to her properly, without becoming angry. It felt like my world was ripped in two and I couldn't find the thread to sew it back up. Over time I began to blame myself and still do in some ways. Now those feelings of mistrust are resurfacing and I need to close them off or I'll be right back in that situation again and my head and heart can't take it.

Connor spoke "Look, I'll do it. Or at least I'll get someone to do it. I won't listen to anything on the files because I don't want to know. Whether it's good news or bad, that's your business. You'll need to give me a few days, I'm not back on duty until Monday and text over her number" Connor said, in reluctant agreement.

When Connor said that he would help me, the tears ran down my cheek. I raised a hand and wiped them away, just before they could drop on my jumper and spoil another item of clothing today. I grabbed my phone and typed Beth's phone number into the text box addressed to Connor. I held it in my hand for a moment, reflecting on the words Connor used. Would it really help to know? I had come this far and hit send.

"Thank you, Connor" was all I could muster.

"No problem, now finish your beer, we're meeting Chris in ten minutes, and you know what a dick he becomes when people are late" no more words were needed.

I raised the half full can, once more to my lips and drained the remaining beer down my throat, I felt like a huge weight had been lifted off my shoulders. Finally, I would know the truth, and Beth will never find out that I had spied on her in such a personal way. I just hope that I find out that my wife is faithful and still in love with me and that I'd created an awful imaginary situation in my head all this time.

We both jumped up from the garden chairs and dashed through the house, Connor locking up as we went. Walking out of the front door and reaching the bottom of the street, I realised I forgot my jacket.

"Mate. I've left my jacket in your dining room" with a sorry Connor expression on my face, knowing fine well that I meant to leave it there, so I didn't have to carry it with me.

"You don't need it, it's boiling, and it makes you look like a farmer anyway" He laughed.

"Yeah ok, let's go" I agreed, as he was kind of right.

# CHAPTER 7
# THE CALL BACK

I woke up on the sofa this Tuesday morning with my laptop still open and the reports and drawings all printed out and sat next to me on the seat. I must have dozed off while catching up on emails. It's not like I had anyone to go to bed with last night, as Beth had stayed over at her Mam's, and I hate sleeping in the big bed alone. It just feels so empty. That's another problem I'll have if the phone recording I get from Connor realise my worst fears. I stayed with her the last time, and it took me months to get over it, to a point that I wasn't constantly suspicious. Those feelings didn't go away completely or else I wouldn't be trying to spy and snoop around in her private life.

I needed to have a shower and wash off the shame of sleeping on the sofa, while I have a perfectly fine super king bed upstairs that I could have used. I pulled myself up from the sofa, I must have been tired last night, as I hadn't even bothered to recline the sofa before sleeping. I headed out to the hallway and noticed some envelopes poking through the inside of my letter box. I never checked for any mail being delivered when I got back from Claire's last night. So, this must be Monday's mail, as our postman doesn't come around until about lunch time, if we're lucky. When I was a kid, I can remember the post being delivered before I left for school. I guess everything has become lazier over the years, including me.

Pulling the post from its restraints I flicked through them. It was the usual stuff like the local pizza place leaflet, some marketing bullshit and a Capital One letter addressed to me. This must be the credit card statement for the card I took out for Beth but have never used myself. I threw the mail on the radiator cover. That's the general place everything goes. Until Beth nags me to tidy up, which happens every couple of weeks. I headed up the stairs, feeling the soft carpet between my bare toes. It was a stark contrast to the cold tiled hallway floor and felt much better. We only tiled the floor for ease of cleaning, as it's much easier to mop up any footprints opposed to trying to clean them from a carpet. And shoes were banned from going upstairs.

I turned on the shower and then removed my t shirt and shorts that I'd slept in, while I gave the water a chance to heat up. Throwing them in the washing basket, which is now starting to overflow. No doubt that will be another ticking off from Beth, that I hadn't done any washing while she was at her Mother's for the evening. I placed my fingertips under the running water and could feel the droplets hitting them finally turning from cold to warm. So, with that, I jumped in and got washed and freshened up.

After getting dried and dressed for the office, I had to dash as I was running slightly late. So, I headed down the stairs, quickly rammed my laptop and reports into my bag and headed off down the drive.

The journey was again, a blur of traffic and red lights. Made even more difficult that I'd left the house later than I normally would. Just as I was pulling in from the main street, my phone rang, and for some reason I must have turned off the Bluetooth, as it didn't connect to the wireless system in my car. I couldn't answer it as I was pulling into my "Director" parking space and the rings stopped. I grabbed my phone and the number I didn't recognise. As I was racking my brain trying to work out who could be calling, it rang again and shocked me to the point that the phone went flying into the air, hitting the roof on the inside of my car. I just managed to catch it, like a Samsung juggler, and hit answer raising the phone to my ear.

"Hello, it's DI Morrison of Northumbria police can I ask your na……" In my nervous haste I cut across him before he could finish his question.

"Oh, hello umm sir. I thought you had forgotten to ring me back" in a fumbling idiot sentence, like I was back to being ten years old and caught stealing sweets from the local shop.

"As I'm sure you can appreciate, we have been extremely busy trying to find a murderer and I just never got round to calling you back yesterday" He had a booming voice and I'd clearly pissed this guy off, unintentionally. Judging by his voice, I had a mental picture of a big guy in his mid-forties. He must have been the one picking up Bibby from Frankie's house yesterday evening. "Sorry sir, I didn't mean anything by it, I'm not used to talking to police officers" That was my attempt to calm the situation.

"It's Detective Inspector Morrison and not Officer! And your name is?" I had again, unintentionally ruffled this guy's feathers.

"Yes, sorry about that. Can I remain anonymous for now? I'm not even sure you'll need my information anymore". I really don't want to end up with our house sprayed with the words "Grass" across it.

"Yes sir. My associate tells me that you have some information about the night that Ben Stapleton was found dead?" That settled my nervous down that I didn't have to give my name.

"Go on sir, tell me everything and I will remain silent throughout and take notes. I may need to ask you some question at the end."

"Well, me and a couple of friends were drinking in the Odd Fellows on Saturday night. Ben was in there standing at the bar with a friend, I couldn't tell you the guy's name, sorry."

"Had you seen Ben with this 'friend' before?" He asked, almost aggressively.

"Erm yeah I think so, but I don't know who he is" Damn, I shouldn't have even called as I don't have much information to tell.

"Okay go on" he said.

"Ben seemed in high spirits. He left the pub at around eleven o'clock maybe a little later. It was about thirty minutes after that before we left, and I never saw him again. I obviously just assumed he had gone home. I left at eleven thirty and crossed over the metal bridge to walk home."

"Which metal bridge is this sir?" He interrupted me and I got a shock.

"Oh, the one at Cox Green, little foot bridge" I replied nervously.

"Okay I see" He added.

"On my route I saw a parked car on the opposite riverbank with its lights shining toward the water."

"And on which side was this?" The Inspector asked.

"On the same side as the pub" I must remember to include details!

"Okay can you describe the car to me? Make, model, colour etc?" He seemed a bit bored of me now.

"It looked like a big car and a dark colour, but I couldn't be certain on the make or colour of the vehicle. I had been drinking quite a lot on Saturday and my recollection might be a bit hazy. I didn't think of it to be anything to worry about, as that's quite a spot for couples to park up. So, I kept walking and I needed to pee, so I went behind a bush and that's when I saw Bibby."

"Who is 'Bibby'?" He is very bored now!

"Sorry, Paul Robertson running past me, Bibby is his nickname. He didn't see me and again, I wouldn't have thought it was odd, but he was running in the opposite direction from his home."

"And where is this famous Mr Bibby's home then?" I could tell by the tone of his voice he was running out of patience.

"He lives in the flats just along from the Biddick Inn" I couldn't for life of me remember the street name.

"Yes, I know where you mean. What happened next Sir?" The Inspector really wanted to move things along now.

"Well, I got home about 12:15am and that's all I know" I felt exhausted.

"Ok thank you for bringing this to our attention. Are you ok for me to ask you couple of question in relation to the events of Saturday night?" His voice had calmed down now, but still held that deep and booming tone of authority.

"Yes of course" I had relaxed now that I had finally told the police my information, it felt good to finally release the tension that I'd been carrying for the last few days.

"Ok Sir. Firstly, who were you with on Saturday night?"
"Connor Mount and Chris Dobson" I quickly replied.
"How much would you say that you had to drink on

Saturday?" This guy was good, his questions were rolling off his tongue, just as fast as I could answer them.

"I would say about nine pints, but I couldn't be sure" I lied, I had way more than that, but I'd already gave my answer now. It felt like when you get the same questions from your doctor and you almost always half the amount before telling them.

"That's ok Sir, could you describe what Ben was wearing when you saw him?" God more questions?!

"Umm, dark jeans, a white or light t shirt and a khaki-coloured jacket I think, but I can't be sure" If he had asked what Jade, the young barmaid was wearing, I could have told him everything she had on, precisely.

"Are you ok to continue Sir?" In that deep voice again that makes me nervous.

"Yes, I have some time before I need to go into the office" I lied for the second time today to a police officer, sorry, Detective Inspector.

"Could you tell me again where the car was that you had seen on your journey home?"

"It was about halfway between the two bridges, there is a little car park there" I could answer questions like that

all day long, we used to go to that car park so often that
I could have drove there blind folded.

"Are you sure you saw Paul Robertson running that
night?" His voice had changed slightly while asking
that question. Like he already knew the answer before
asking it.

"Yes, it was him, the clothing and the scar on his face"
It was him, I know it was him, and DI Morrison knew it
was too.

"Thanks for answering those questions, Sir. I know
your recollection of the events might be clouded by the
alcohol, but it was of great importance that you have
come forward with this information" his voice had
changed again, it's a more settled and calming approach.
"Just one last thing Sir before I let you get off to work.
It's not in relation to your statement, but more about
something that you said earlier. You said, I'm not even
sure you'll need my information now. Can you elaborate
on that sentence please?" His last question had caught
me off guard slightly.

"Well, I was in the park with my nephew yesterday teatime
and I saw you and another officer pick up Bibby, sorry,
Paul Robertson from Frankie Jacksons house" I hoped
that I hadn't come across as being nosy or anything.

"We did pick up Paul from Frankie's house, that part is correct. But we picked him up from there this morning at 6:00am, after we received an anonymous tip off. So, whoever you had seen yesterday, wasn't us".

This makes no sense to me, if it wasn't them, then who was it?

"Oh, I'm sorry, I just saw him being led into a black Range Rover by two smartly dressed guys and assumed it was the police". My worrying nervousness had resurfaced at this point, and I could feel a sheen of sweat forming on my forehead and across the back of my neck.

"I'm not sure you are up to speed on the force's budgets Sir, but driving around in Range Rovers isn't common practice. As I said, we have picked up Paul for questioning and are holding him here for the time being. We may need to get you down the station at some point to make an official statement, but I'll be in touch about that. Until then, can you tell me anything about the Range Rover and the two men involved?" he probably told me too much information at this point, but I could tell from his phone manner that he liked to show off and feeding me this information, was his verbal way of flexing his pecks.

"I'm really sorry Inspector, I was a hundred yards away. All I know, is that it was a black Range Rover and the two guys looked like detectives. One was a large guy, more muscle than fat, if you know what I mean. Maybe mid to late forties and bald. The other guy was about the same age, tall and slim. I'm sorry I can't be of more help. Maybe Frankie's neighbours got a closer look. Sorry" This has gone too far already, God knows who those guys were, but I now suspect that it is some local gangster thugs, and I want nothing to do with any of it at all. "Thanks for your information so far Sir and we'll let you get back to your day. If you remember anything, please ring me directly on this number, I'll be in touch. Goodbye" and with that the phone went dead.

What did he mean by "so far"? I have nothing else to give him and even if I did, I'm not sure that I would bring it forward to the police now. I just need to put this behind me for now and try to get some normality back to my life.

I threw my phone into my laptop bag, I grabbed a tissue and wiped my brow and neck of the sweat, that ten-minute phone call created and threw it onto the back seat. Beth always insisted on using her car if we went anywhere as according to her, my car was a skip on wheels. Her words exactly. I headed into the office, and again the parasites started circling.

"Hi Boss, didn't think you were ever going to get out of your car" indicating that they had been spying eyes from the office windows. I get no peace from these people. I couldn't hold back the lashing this guy was about to get.

"Why don't you try and do some work instead of licking my arse every second of the day?!" I didn't wait for a response, I left him standing in the middle of the open plan office and headed to my personal office so I could catch my breath, but that didn't last long as HR Hannah's assistant was walking straight towards me. "Hi, I need to spe…"

"Good morning, sir, Bill from finance is waiting on line one, he says its urgent" thank God for Julie interrupting Hannah's little lapdog, she just saved my life for a short while at least.

I darted into the office and closed the door. Sat behind my desk and picked up the desk phone. "Hi Bill, what seems to be the problem?" the phone was silence.

"Bill are you there?" I tried again.

The voice came back "Bills not in today, but Julie is" followed by giggles.

"You are a life saver" as I continued our chat, while we sat separated only by the glass wall of my office.

"I know, I know. You'll say I'm amazing and whatever else. Also, if you look down to your right, you'll see that I made you a coffee too, in your favourite mug" she said with a note of maternal love in her voice.

"Thank you, Julie," I looked at her through the glass, she didn't speak, but span around in her seat and blew me a kiss.

The rest of the day went without a hitch. I managed to get the monthly reports sent off to the board and the numbers had improved month on month since I took over. It had nothing to do with me, but if they want to throw credit my way, I'll take it when it comes. As I was packing up for the day. I text Beth, as I hadn't heard anything from her since yesterday morning. "Are you coming home tonight?" I waited a couple of moments and saw those two ticks turn blue which means she's read it.

"Yeah, but about 8, need a bikini for the spa on Saturday, so going shopping after work" I didn't bother to reply to that, feeling if I don't reply that she will get the picture that I'm not happy about it.

As I left the office, Julie was sitting in her car. I made a director decision to get Julie her own parking space, so that she could get closer to the building, but mainly to piss off everyone else that wanted one. She raised her hand in a wave to me as I walked past the front of her car. Her window was slightly down and since I had nowhere to be really, I walked over and asked if she fancied going for a drink. It wasn't anything unusual, we often did it, maybe once a month.

"Sorry sweetie, not tonight, I have to take Jake to his swimming lesson, maybe tomorrow though?" That was reasonable enough.

"That would great, see you tomorrow, I owe you one" I said, feeling slightly disheartened by the rejection, but I understood the reasoning completely.

"More than one!" She shouted out of her window as she pulled away from her very own parking space.

I headed home and this time checked to see if the post was sticking out of the letter box on the inside of our front door. Just two things this time, one was our joint account bank statement, I could see it from the black horse in the top corner of the envelope and the other was a note from our window cleaner, saying that he'd been today and needed paying. It cost me ten pounds every time he came and I'm positive that the outside of the windows have never seen soapy water in the five years that we've lived here. Basically, just a charity. I may as well sponsor a donkey, from one of those

TV adverts with the money. The donkey might do a better job of cleaning these windows. I added these unopened envelopes to the ever-growing mound of unopened envelopes on the radiator cover. I threw down my laptop bag at the bottom of the stairs and decided to make myself a sandwich for tea, as Beth would be a couple of hours before she got home. Opening the fridge, I couldn't help but think back to Connors sparse fridge and how I was going to be on the same diet as him, at least for tonight. Picking out a few bits I made my sandwich, then returned to the fridge to grab a beer. After the day I've had, I think I deserve a cold one.

I was going to lay in front of the TV and see if there was any football on, but I decided to sit at the breakfast bar to eat and wait for Beth to come home.

But when the clock struck 10:00pm, I couldn't keep my eyes open and decide to go to bed. Still no sign of Beth.

# CHAPTER 8
# THE NIGHT OUT

Me and Connor approach the big old wooden door of the pub which was painted in British racing car green. Judging from the paintwork, it had a coat of paint every year it had been there. I always thought that the door might only be small but doubled in size from the multiple layers of paint. I grabbed Connor by the forearm, which caused him to spin and face me in alarm.

"Listen mate, please don't say anything to Chris about our chat earlier. You know what he's like and I can't deal with his constant shit all night" I already knew that Connor wouldn't say a word about it, but I had to make the statement anyway, just so that I was sure in my head. "Of course, I won't say anything. Come on, I need a drink and Chris is already inside, who could miss that fucking car!" as the last word escaped his mouth, Connor had turned and headed in.

I stayed outside and lit a cigarette. I haven't smoked in years, but decided to grab a pack from the shop earlier today. Although that was a nightmare, as my joint account card had declined after numerous attempts at trying to pay, both contactless and by inserting my card. It got to the point where I started to become embarrassed, that the man serving me thought I couldn't pay and didn't have the £10.20 funds in my bank account. Finally, I gave up on our joint card and had to use my personal one. That card was forever letting me down, I was constantly holding up queues of people at cash machines. I should just bite the bullet and order a new one.

As I inhaled the dreaded smoke, I coughed and looked like a guy who was trying to look cool and failing miserably. Thankfully no one else was outside. I looked at Chris's Car, bright green, almost luminous Porsche. When he bought it, I got the whole explanation about what type it was, horsepower and how much it cost. And I can't remember anything he told me. But it makes him happy, and I guess his bankers bonus paid for it. He must be leaving it here over night and getting a taxi home, as I've never known Chris to be in a pub and not drink, ever.

Once I'd had a couple of draws of the cigarette, I instantly regretted buying them. I threw the cigarette on the floor and stubbed it out with the sole of my muddied trainer, then took the pack from my pocket and threw them in the river. It was a stupid idea to buy them and one I will probably do again sometime.

I pushed open the heavy, severely painted door and went through. Walking past the gents toilet on route to the bar. I scanned the bar area looking for Connor and Chris. No sign of Connor, but Chris was leaning against the bar chatting to Ben and Ben's friend, who I didn't know. As Chris lifted his head up from his conversation and caught my eyesight, I lifted a hand, in a silent way of saying hello. I headed over to the bar.

"What're you drinking?" Chris asked.

"Pint please mate, and better get one for Connor, although I have no idea where he has gone" I responded "There's the puff there" Chris had a way with words, how he became so successful at the bank, I'll never know.

I turned and saw Connor walking in, he must have been to the toilet. I said hello to Ben and his friend, I grabbed my drink and headed over to the pool table. Connor and Chris came over a few seconds later after Chris had got the remaining drinks and paid Gill for the privilege.

"I see you've brought your flash motor out tonight" Connor said to Chris.

"Yeah, I got changed at work and came straight here, I've been here an hour already, waiting for you two muppets. I'll either ask Gill for a ride home or grab a taxi"

I had forgotten that Gill lives on the other side of town, near Chris's house, not quite as posh as Chris's pad, but it was on the same estate.

"Should we play?" I said with an air of confidence, they both know how good I am at pool. It's probably from all the college days when I should have been in lectures. But instead spent three years in the pub and my pool skills were second to none ever since. That was the only thing I learned in those years.

"I'm not playing you for money" Connor said.

"Me neither" Chris added, even though he knows that a couple of pounds lost here and there was never going to break his bank account. This is a guy, when at the age of thirty, bought his house outright and was offered one million pounds from the bank to buy him out of his final salary pension. And he refused.

"You lads are soft as fuck." I added as I started to set the balls up.

After a few games of pool, I won them all, and a few more rounds of beers, the conversation becomes varied. We normally get the pleasantries out of the way in the first hour or so. Such things like 'How's the family? How's work going?' etc. then it generally moves onto

Chris having a dig at Connor for being single and almost every time ends up with Chris asking Connor if he's gay. To Chris, being single at our age wasn't a normal situation. He says things like.

"So, what happened to the last girl, did she find your gay porn stash and finally realise that you enjoy cock more than her?" and Connors reply is always "You're just jealous because I turned you down" I always laugh at that, and Chris is always left fuming.

It had reached 9:30pm and I was trying to remember a film that I watched the other night, I couldn't for the life of me remember what happened in it, or who was in it. But I do remember that it was good. The lads had no clue what I was talking about, so I tried to Google the tv listings for last week. I typed as far as TV Lis and my phone died.

"Shit I should have put it on charge for a bit, while I was at your house" I said looking up at Connor. Chris couldn't help himself at this point.

"Oh, that's you in the bad books tomorrow, you won't be texting the boss letting her know what time you'll be home" and he burst into laughter at his own joke.

"Fuck off Chris, and it's your round" I couldn't be bothered with his crap tonight.

"Ok, Ok, I must have touched a nerve" and with that he went off to the bar and ordered three more pints. While he was gone Connor sat down next to me

"Are you ok? You seem on edge" Connor asked with an air of concern.

"Yes, mate I'm fine, I'm just a little wound up about the whole Beth situation" I was trying to retain my composure. "You'll know the truth sooner or later, try not to let it bother you." Connor said reassuringly.

He had just finished speaking when Chris arrived back at the table with more drinks.

"Anyway, Beth wouldn't want you texting her tonight, I'm sure she's busy enough" When I heard Chris say that I looked directly at Connor, had he told him? Connor looked at me in a way that showed me, he knew what my look was for. And he just shook his head from side to side. Connor hadn't said a word to Chris about our conversation earlier.

"What the fuck does that mean?!" I hadn't meant it to come out in a threatening tone, but it did.

"Oh nothing, I didn't mean anything by it, just that she might be busy. I don't know, maybe planning for your birthday" I could hear in his voice that I had caught him off guard, and in that moment, I realised that I was the one taking things to heart. He genuinely meant nothing by his words, other than to maybe wind me up. I need to calm down.

Another round of generally talking crap and more beer flowing. Connor had gotten up and was chatting to Jade, the glamorous young barmaid. She was Gill's niece and had been working here for the last few months. Just working the weekends for some extra cash while she was studying at university. From my seat I could see them talking and her becoming more flirtatious with Connor as the moments passed. Her hand resting against his. The way she was laughing at every comment he made. Not that I could hear what he was saying to her, but I've known Connor for years and he isn't as funny as she is making out. As she swept back her light brown hair from the side of her face, Gill had walked up to Jades side, mumbling something in her ear. This was Gills attempt to diffuse the situation. As soon as Gill moved her mouth away from Jades ear. Jade proceeded to walk out from around the bar and start collecting in empty glasses. It was nearly 10:30pm at this point and this was the first time tonight that any empties had been collected. Yes, Jade was beautiful, but she wasn't proactive. As she walked over to our table, her hips swaying from side to side, wearing light grey gym pants and a white t shirt, that was too short, so that her toned stomach was on show to all the fellas that cared to look. Maybe it was a fashion thing, to wear short t shirts? I have no idea. But what I do know is that her hips swaying, wasn't for my benefit, but it was for Connors. Who had remained standing at the bar and had the best view in the house of Jade's bottom. He wasn't trying to hide where he was looking either.

During her thirty seconds of Connor seduction, Chris had come back from the toilet and was sitting next to me "For all Connor is a fag, he gets the pick of the women. Have you seen her? She's gorgeous" Chris couldn't find the strength to give Connor a compliment, without having a dig at him in the same breath.

"I know, but in a few months, he'll be onto his next victim" as I tried to join in with Chris's digs.

"Yeah, but he gets a lot of practice" and the laugher started. Both of us sitting quite drunk now and giggling like school children. Connor then plonked down some more beer and added three shot glasses to the table "Courtesy of the hot barmaid" while pointing down at the tiny glasses, filled with clear liquid. As we all raised the glasses to our lips, my hope of it only containing water was short lived. As the smell of Vodka wafted up my nostrils. No turning back now, and my lips parted, and the clear liquid flowed into my mouth and with one quick gulp it was safely on its journey to my stomach and ultimately to an even worse hangover in the morning. As I slammed the glass onto the table, I heard the other two glasses touch down seconds after. The burn started, only lasting a short while, but strong enough for me to screw my face up and looking over Connors shoulder at Jade, she was laughing at our expense. After that Chris made his goodbyes to us and started stumbling towards the exit door. Gill shouted over.

"Chris, Chris wait. Do you want a lift? I'll be an hour yet though" she called. As Chris continued his exit, shouting back.

"No thanks, Taxi" and the heavy door closed with him now on the other side.

"For all he talks shit, he's actually a good guy at heart" I was talking about Chris to Connor.

"Yeah, he is, but he can't hold his drink, a bit like you" Connors turn to have a dig.

"I see you've got another girl in mind" as my eyes darted up to look over the bar towards Jade.

"Yeah, she seems fun" Connor being as vague as ever. "Anyway, enough about her, how are you holding up?" He always had to check and make sure everyone was ok, maybe that's why he was so good in the force. If every Police officer had the same mentality, then maybe the world would be a better place.

"I'm good mate, honestly. Tonight, was just what I needed. Just nice to unwind you know". I sighed.

"Yeah, I know what you mean" He tapped my shoulder in his comforting way. It was getting close to 11:15pm and I had just seen Ben saying his goodbyes to Jade and Gill, he turned and waved a hand in the air towards me. I lifted a hand, and the silent goodbye was complete. I have noticed over the years that guys don't necessarily need to speak to communicate with each other. A signal or hand gesture I sufficient in most greetings or farewells. I put my theory to the test, as I lift my beer to my mouth and took a big mouthful, watching the remains of my glass run dry and then setting the pint glass, back against the wooden table. With my cheek bulging with Beer, I looked at Connor and pointed to my watch and then pointed towards the door.

"Stay for one more, Jades got thirty minutes left here and I'm taking her home. I don't fancy waiting here on my own" Connor said. My theory was a success.

I swallowed down the rest of my beer that was trapped in my cheek's seconds earlier and finally able to speak

"Ok, but you're paying" With that Connor went back to see Jade at the bar and ordered our last drinks of the night. After a few minutes of him flirting again, he returned, and we chatted about anything and everything until Gill shouted up.

"Come on you two, we're closed!"

With that, we got up and I placed my now empty pint glass on the bar and said goodbye to Gill. Me, Connor, and Jade headed outside. And Jade said her very first words to me.

"My cars over there if you want a lift, I can drop you off while I drop off Connor" It was very kind of her to offer and if she thinks I believe her about only dropping off Connor, she is quite young and naïve. She obviously doesn't know what's going to happen in a few months when she tries to take the relationship to the next level, and he puts a blockade in front of her. Maybe I could be wrong, and, on some level, I hope I am. It would be nice to have another couple to go out with for food etc and Beth would prefer it over going out with Dylan and his well-groomed bride.

"Thanks for the offer, but I think I'll walk home, looks like a nice night, have fun you two" I added the last part to make both of them embarrassed, but I knew it would only work on her.

"I'll text you through the week about that thing, ok?" Connor said.

"Thanks mate, and don't forget, poker night, my place next Saturday".

With that I headed to the metal bridge and from behind me I could hear her car doors close behind them and the engine start up.

# CHAPTER 9
# BETH'S HOME

I was walking bare foot on moss covered stones, heading towards a waterfall, hearing the water cascading down through the valley it had carved in the mountainside. Getting closer and the noise of the splashing spring getting ever louder. As I reached the edge and looked over, I could see the bubbles from where the waterfall had ended as it hit the pool, sending ripples across to all sides. I stretched out my arms and let my body fall. My vision closing in around me, no longer able to see the waterfall or the moss-covered edges, only blue, getting ever closer.

Just before I hit the pool of water I was startled into the land of the living, breathing heavy and sitting upright in the darkness, covered with a light sheen of sweat across my face and torso and my lower half covered with the thin white sheets of our bed. I could still hear the waterfall, those droplets crashing down. As I turned to my side, now looking toward the bedroom door, I could see a light shining under it, illuminating the carpet.

I grabbed my phone, it was 1:10am. Had Beth just gotten back? I rolled out of bed, and headed to the door, the waterfall was getting louder. Opening the bedroom door, steam clouds hitting my cheeks. As the sound got louder. I headed out onto the landing, the bathroom door was wide open and the waterfall sounds, weren't a waterfall at all, it was the shower. I walked over to the bathroom, still naked from my momentary sleep. As I entered the bathroom, the shower was running, I had expected to see Beth, naked under the water, washing off some new type of shampoo, or whatever else she does in there. No one was standing under the water.

As I lowered my head I saw Beth's red hair, she was curled up and sitting on the shower floor. I have no idea how long she had been there but judging by the amount of steam in the bathroom and spreading across the landing, I would guess at least thirty minutes or so. She hadn't noticed me standing there and I could hear beyond the cascading water that she was crying. Her arms wrapped around her body, covering her naked skin from no one. No one else was here, just me and her. Why was she in here alone and clearly upset? Why wasn't she in the comforting arms of her loving husband? I reached around the shower door. I could see that she had her eyes closed and didn't know that I was there. I was intending to place a hand on her, but instead I reached for the shower tap and slowing turned it to off. As the water came to a sudden stop, her eyes darted open and scanned the room. Finally settling on me standing there. She looked up, with mascara streaks down her cheeks. She looked so pitiful in that moment. She didn't speak, as I reached for a towel to get her dried off. She stood up and before I could wrap the towel around her, she wrapped both hands around me and began crying again, this time into my chest. I draped the towel over her back, and we stood still for the next twenty minutes, wrapped together. I had so many questions that I wanted to ask, but I couldn't bring myself to speak and break her grip on me.

With her head buried into my chest, I could hear that her crying had subsided. Just the odd whimper and sniffle of her nose coming and going. Then it was Beth that broke the silence, never lifting her head for a moment.

"I guess I owe you an explanation?"

"Yes, but only when you are ready" I replied.

The silence continued for a while longer, while we stood on the cold tiled bathroom floor, both nude but feeling nothing sexual. I felt her fingertips loosen the grip she held on my back and her head starting to lift from my chest.

"Ok, I'll tell you everything, but can we go and sit in the kitchen, and I'll make you a coffee" The trembling in her voice had subsided and she was almost in a calm state now.

"Sure darling, I'll just grab our robes and we can go downstairs." I left Beth in the bathroom and went to grab our robes from the back of our bedroom door.

I quickly grabbed my phone and text Julie 'I won't be in tomorrow, don't feel too good. Sorry for the time of this text. I'll make it up to you x' hitting send as I put it back down on the bedside table.

I headed back to Beth and held out her robe for her to slide her arms in. She gave me a little kiss as I tied the robe around her waist. I threw on my robe as Beth was walking down the stairs.

As I got to the kitchen, Beth had her back to me, standing over the coffee machine, adding the ground coffee to the filter cup. I thought we would be in for a long night, and if we aren't having instant coffee, then it certainly looks like I was right. I sat on one of the breakfast bar stools and swung myself from right to left, waiting for the aroma of coffee to be emitting from the machine. It felt like it was taking ages, I was growing impatient, and just want to get to the bottom of the issue, whatever it may be. Just before I was about to ask the question, Beth turned on her heels and with two steaming mugs, one in each hand. Walking over to the breakfast bar, her wet red hair clinging to sides of her face and her robe becoming slightly looser than when I'd tied it, showing off just enough cleavage. I could throw those mugs away and have her right here and now. She looked so beautiful my heart ached. But this wasn't the place or the time for it. She had something important to tell me and my pent-up urges can wait.

As she set the mugs down on the breakfast bar and pulled herself onto a stool sitting opposite me. I took a sip as she just stared over the breakfast bar, looking me directly into my eyes. I brought the mug down from my lips and said,

"What's going on Beth?" I ask quietly.

"Ok, what I'm about to tell you isn't easy for me to say, or for you to hear. But before I start, I need to know that whatever you hear that you are willing to sit and listen and I hope you can forgive me" As the last words escaped her mouth, I saw a single tear roll down her cheek.

My heart sank when she asked me to forgive her, before telling me what to forgive her for. In that moment, I thought my worst fears had been realised. She was having an affair, and I didn't need the recording from

Connor to find that out. I was about to hear it straight from her lying lips. I composed myself, masking my true feelings before replying.

"Listen Beth, whatever you are about to tell me, I'm ready to hear and will try and forgive whatever it is you've done. I can promise to try" I know deep in my heart that I want to forgive her for cheating on me again, but I know I can't. I will have to move on.

"Ok please listen. When I have told you that I've been going to see my Mam, that part is true. But it wasn't to help her with shopping or around the house. My mother had been scammed out of a lot of money, thirty thousand pounds to be precise. She had met a new man online and paid for him to come and visit her. But obviously he didn't show up. That money was what my father had left her to live on. That was my dad's money, and she blew it on some guy she's never even seen in person" The tears were rolling down her cheeks at this point. I didn't want to say anything, as I had promised to listen.

"So, she remortgaged the house to put the money back, in case I found out. But then she ended up using all the cash to keep up the mortgage payments. When it ran out and the bank were going to repossess the house. She couldn't get a loan as her credit rating is as bad as mine and the missed payments didn't help. She started borrowing money from Tommy Carter, you know who I mean?" I nodded in agreement, still not breaking my silence. Everyone had heard of Tommy Carter.

"Ok, so she started off borrowing a small amount, just to keep on top of things, but then the borrowing continued. She owed him twenty-five grand. So not only did she lose the money that my dad left her, but she also had that amount to pay back as well. I only found all of this out a few weeks ago, please believe me" She was talking so fast it was hard to keep up, the words spilling out one after another. Something she said in the last part about her mother, that she owed him twenty-five grand and not owes him the money, didn't sit right with me and I had to break my vow of silence.

"What do you mean, she owed him?" I said with a quizzical tone.

"Well, I paid off the twenty-five thousand from our joint account, I couldn't let it continue. That's why I've been selling clothes and whatever I can, just to keep enough money in there, for you to use as I know you don't check the statements and I was going to put it all back, I promise" She was shaking and crying as the words flowed from her mouth.

"So that's why my card was declined in the shop on Saturday?" Were the only words I could find.

"Yes. I'm so sorry, the account is empty" she stared down at the table, not lifting her head to make eye contact.

"How did you get the money out of the account? You need both signatures for any withdraws from our joint account, if it's over a thousand pounds" I know what I'm saying is correct, as Chris manages our finances at the bank, and it was written into the terms.

"I had to tell Chris, that I needed the withdrawal to buy you a new car for your birthday. That it was going to be a surprise and if there was any way to get around the double signature issue. He sorted it out in a few minutes and promised not to say anything to you". So that was why Chris had made the comment about Beth being busy planning my birthday.

To be fair to Chris, he had kept his word to her and didn't blab anything to me. As she lifted her head and looking into my eyes this time.

"That's not the worst part. After I paid him via Frankie Jackson, as Tommy always uses a middleman, he said that the interest was 100% so the debt wasn't twenty-five thousand, it was fifty grand, and that the debt needs to be settled by no later than Friday or it doubles again. I don't know what to do. We have no more money and I'm not sure that my car is worth that much or I'd sell it"

I could see the genuine look of panic across her face as she relayed this information.

I could involve Connor and get his steer on the situation. But I know that he'll say, don't be stupid and let the Police take care of the situation. I don't need that, and I certainly don't need a lecture right now. If the debt isn't settled, these guys could hurt Beth or me. Even worse, Frankie knows that Claire lives on his estate and if anything happened to her or little James, as a direct result of our actions, I could never forgive myself. I know all about Tommy Carter, he runs a gang of criminals involved in drugs, prostitution, and protection. Even the Odd Fellows has a sign in the window saying, 'Carter Security'. This is a man who kicked a nineteen-year-old to death, all because he lost a game of snooker to him. He did two years of his sentence and from what I heard from Connor, he has a lot of the police force on the payroll. So, if I go to the police, ultimately, he will get off with it and they'll find our bodies hanging from the tallest tree in the woods and another unsolved murder for DI Morrison to deal with.

I sat in silence for the next five minutes, trying to remain calm and not blurt out, just how fucking stupid Beth and her fucking mother had been, but Beth didn't need a scolding right now. She needed help and that's why she told me all of this. The only positive thing I could take from our middle of the night conversation, was that she wasn't having an affair. Beth broke the silence this time "Please say something" in a pleading tone.

"We might not have that money in the joint account, but I have close to twenty thousand in my personal one and I'm sure Chris would help me out with the missing five, I'll speak to Chris in the morning" I had to try and help her.

"Are you sure? I really didn't want to get you involved and I really didn't want any of this, you believe me, right?" Her tears had started again.

"Yes, I'm sure. I hate your mother even more now" I managed to raise a smile at that last part and Beth noticed and a little smile shone through from her sad face.

"I'm so sorry about this mess" She murmured.

"It's ok, well, it's not ok. But it soon will be" She nodded in understanding that just because I was going to sort out this mess, that she was still in the bad books.

"You need to arrange for the payment to be made tomorrow night and it will be me that goes to Frankie's house to drop it off. I know that you aren't telling me everything that happened, or else, why were you sitting in the shower for thirty minutes, maybe even longer. and that's ok, but it must be something that you tell me in the future". There was something else, something worse going on, but if I find out now, I might kill Frankie or Tommy before I make the payment and that wouldn't end well for anyone. She dropped her head and spoke into her coffee cup.

"I promise you, I'll set it up and when this is all over, I'll tell you what happened. I just can't find the words, just yet. But just know that I love you with all my heart" She never lifted her head up for the whole sentence. "I know. Now let's get this mess sorted out and move on with our lives".

With that, I got up and walked around the breakfast bar to where Beth was sitting. Taking her cup from her hand and place them both into the dish washer. I turned back and placed my hands on her shoulders from behind.

"It's going to be alright. I promise. I think we should try at least to get some sleep. We have a busy day tomorrow" while sweeping her wet hair off her shoulder. She didn't say anything more until we had reached the bottom of the stairs, she turned and faced me.

"You do still love me, don't you?" She looked like a little girl staring up at me.

"Of course, I do. How could I ever stop?" and with that we both made our way up the wooden hill for that last time tonight.

# CHAPTER 10
# CALM

Sleep didn't come easy for both of us, the moments I managed to doze off, I was woken by Beth wimpering. into her pillow, with her back turned towards me. Beth must have only slept for an hour for the whole night. When it was 08:10am I was woken again, by Beth's voice, as she was on the phone outside of the bedroom door, telling her boss that she was unwell and will try and make it into the office later. I realised that this was the first time that Beth had missed her pre-work workout at the gym in months. When she re-entered the bedroom and walked around the foot of the bed, I could see that she was still naked. She reached her side and crawled back under the covers as I pretended to sleep. When her head fell onto her pillow and her back again turned towards me. I rolled onto my side and for the first time since Saturday morning my hand fell down against the soft, but firm skin of her upper thigh. I was content in that moment. I ran my hand gently over her pale skin and she placed her hand on top of mine. "I love you" came from her lips, as the light from the morning sun, shone across the white covers and landing upon her silhouette. "I love you too. When this is all sorted, we can get back to normal" I could stay here forever. This was my happy place.

"You need to arrange the drop off for tonight" I returned our attention to problem at hand. "I have already text Frankie, he says it has to be me, dropping it off" and she starting to cry again, she was trying to hide it. But I know when my wife is upset, and this was one of those times.

"Tell him that it's me or no money!"

I wasn't in the mood to negotiate with a prick like him and I certainly wasn't sending Beth back in that house. God knows what happened the last time. I suddenly realised that she must have been there last night. And why spend so much time washing herself in the shower. My blood was beginning to boil, I need to compose myself and not think about the possibilities, until this is over. Then I'll find out exactly what happened.

"I'll text him now" as she shifted in bed and propped herself up against the head of the bed, my hand fell from her thigh, and I left it laying on the sheets.

I could see the concentration on her face as she typed away on her phone. The light emitting from it highlighting her exposed top half to the room. The moment she said, "Ok I've done it", her phone vibrated and lighted up once again.

"He's said 'Just you and the money 6:30pm, anyone else and it's off'" I nodded, and she wrote back telling him that it was a deal. I need to speak with Chris about the extra five grand or I'm going to turn up at Frankie's light on the cash and I'm assuming that isn't going to go down well.

As she put down her phone on the bedside table, she slowly moved her body under the covers and finding a comfortable spot, with her head resting against my chest. I lay there staring at the white ceiling as my hands ran through her silky, flowing hair. I couldn't shift my gaze and must have been lay there in this position for the next thirty minutes. If something was to go wrong tonight, this might be my last chance to feel the warmth and loving touch of my wife and I wanted to saviour it. Beth broke my daydream, not lifting her head from my chest, she spoke "Are you sure Chris will help?"

"I'm sure, if he thinks that I'm in his debt, he'll love it". What I didn't tell Beth was that I planned to take Chris along, not into the house. But if anything happened and I didn't come out for whatever reason. Chris's rage would take over and maybe a few heads would go through some coffee tables afterwards. Plus, I don't think my nerves would allow me to drive.

"Need to talk about money, when are you free?" was my text Chris.

"Free after 4pm everything ok?" Was his response.

"I need to borrow some cash, meet you at the bank?" short messages are the way guys communicate, straight to the point and no fluffing around the issue.

"Bank mate, see you then". I sent him back a thumbs up emoji and I know Chris will be good for the cash.

"Ok, I'm meeting Chris at four o'clock this afternoon and I'll go straight to Frankie's afterwards" I was trying to remain calm throughout the whole situation. In some attempt to reassure Beth that her husband can take care of her and that she doesn't need to worry. On the inside, my stomach was turning, and I feared for both our lives for what the night may turn into.

"Can we go out for breakfast? I know we don't have any money left, but I've got a little cash in my handbag" I had to laugh at that. Here we were, only a couple of days ago, living a very comfortable lifestyle and no worries of money issues at all. Now we sit, with all our money either given away or very soon to be given away to some gangster, for no other reason, other than her mother had fucked our lives. I laughed at the irony of the situation. Now we were going to have breakfast with our last available scraps of cash. Beth even smiled in that moment as we both realised how dumb at all sounds.

"Of course, let's go and blow our cash on a fry up".

I watched Beth getting dressed in-between her saying "Keep your eyes to yourself Mr".

I watched her selecting her outfit, a summer style dress and white converse trainers. Beautiful and cool all wrapped up in one amazing bundle. As she was now fully clothed and sitting at her dressing table, brushing something on her face, I got out of bed, found some underwear, and grabbed my jeans and a t-shirt. When I was fully clothed and just pulling on my now clean and back to looking like new trainers I turned and saw her tying up her hair into a ponytail. I decided to try and lighten the mood.

"Hey look at you. See you can get ready quickly!"

She rolled her eyes and headed out of the bedroom and down the stairs, with me closely following.

"Can we go now?" As she looked up at me, as I descended the last step on the stairs. I nodded in agreement, and we headed out of the house to her car. She always looks so good driving her Mercedes, with her Gucci sunglasses on and the wind from the open window, splashing against her face.

As we drove along the little country lane, to a little secluded café that we both enjoy, Beth turned and said, "I can sell this and we could make the bank balance look a lot better?" she was referring to her car.

"No, we can't, as I don't want to raise suspicion amongst our friends, if you sell it then the questions will start to flood in, and we need to be able to forget this whole situation in time. I just want our normal life back. Also, you love this car".

"I love you more" As she reached over and squeezed my upper leg. We had made the short journey and Beth spun the car around on the gravel carpark and into a parking space that faced onto the country lane. As Beth was unclipping her seat belt, I saw the black Range Rover drive past. Normally I wouldn't notice things like this, but I could see the two guys in their suits, sitting in the front. At least I now know that it's not DI Morrison anymore. They just drove past, they didn't look our way and in a second or two, they were gone. Now hidden by the hedged verges of the lane.

As we sat down in the window seats, just out of reach from the now burning, morning sun. I don't fair too well in warm climates, and I tend to burn more than I ever would tan. More of a white to red and back to white, kind of guy. So, I was glad that Beth picked this table, as it looked like the only one in the shade, as I scanned my eyes across the room. I knew what Beth was going to order, she always get the same thing. I think she is frightened that if she changes her order and it's not as delicious as her usual, then she would have let herself down. Just then she told the guy, who had suddenly and silently appeared to my left, that she would have poached eggs on sourdough toast. As she was ordering I had to check the man's feet. Seriously, he was silent in his approach, and I thought he must be wearing slippers or something. But no, just a pair of well-worn in, black brogues. I then ordered a full English breakfast, with everything on it, except mushroom. I was ordering like this could be our last meal together, but without saying the words we were looking at each other and, in that moment, both knew that we were thinking the same thing.

The food was delicious. As I looked down at our two empty plates that were once full. I probably wouldn't eat again today, at least not until after I'd been to Frankie's. I figure I've left enough time for my food to fully settle, before going over to his place. If I eat anything else closer to the time, I might throw up in Chris's Porsche.

As I paid the bill and Beth headed out to the car. I saw the Range Rover again, through the Victorian leaded windows. This time driving in the other direction. They were obviously on the return journey. Once I paid, with the last of Beth's cash we got in the car and headed towards home. On the journey, Beth spoke.

"Do you mind if I go and see my mam for a little while? I promise, I'm going to see her, this time".

"Yeah, no bother, just drop me off at home. I might try and get some sleep on the sofa. Oh, also, do me a favour and slap her across the face and make sure she knows it's from me?" as I raised a wry smile at me own joke.

And Beth shifted uncomfortably but she could sense I didn't mean it. As Beth pulled to a stop, now outside of our house. I unbuckled my seat beat and leaned in to kiss her on the cheek. We said our goodbyes and she drove off as I entered the house. My phone vibrated and made that little beeping sound, it was Julie. "Hope you're feeling better?" she really is a star.

"Still not great, going to sleep. Thanks" I had to re-read the message I sent her last night, just to make sure I didn't make any mistakes and trip myself up.

"I'll check on you tomorrow" I didn't bother to reply. I was crashing on the sofa at this point, as I put the

TV on for background noise and paying no attention to it at all. As my eyes closed and I drifted off.

The signature entrance for Beth, with her slamming the front door, had again woke me up from my slumber on the sofa. I glanced down at my watch, and it was now two o'clock. Beth strolled into the living room and collapsed on the sofa next to me, grabbing the TV remote she started to flick through the channels, finally settling on some holiday home show. God, I hadn't realised just how bad, midweek day time TV was. Saying that, weekend TV isn't much better. As we lay there on the sofa, neither of us spoke. We both had a lot on our minds, and this was our way of trying in some vain attempt to be normal about the whole thing. Even if it was only short lived. "I'm going to take a shower and get freshened up, are you ok to drop me off in town afterwards?" I needed Beth to give me a lift, as I didn't want to take my car. Although Frankie knew me, he didn't know what I drove so, if something went wrong tonight, at least he wouldn't know when I was visiting Claire and James next week by my car parked out of their house.

"Yes of course I'll drop you off, but how are you going to get home after, well you know what?"

"I'll get a taxi, it's no big deal. But the moment you get home from town, I want you to lock all the doors and windows and have Connor's number ready to ring, should something happen, and I don't return. I'll text you when it's over. OK?"

She nervously nodded in response. When I said that, it was the first time that I let my emotions rise to the surface, I wasn't crying, but I could feel the moisture building up in the bottom of my eye lids as I walked up the stairs for my shower.

As I returned to the living room wearing the same clothes that I left it in, only twenty minutes ago. The only difference being that my hair was slightly damp, and I felt a lot cleaner, although that probably wouldn't be noticed by anyone but me.

"Are you ready?" I must have walked into the living room quietly or Beth was lost in her own thoughts, as she spun towards me, startled by my presence. She was still sitting on the sofa in a shocked daze. I knelt on the floor in front of her, resting a hand on each of her thighs and spoke.

"Please don't worry, this will be over soon. But right now, I need you to be brave, for me. I need you to drive me to the bank now. It's time".

She didn't speak, only gripping my hands with hers. Then we walked through the hall and out of the house, as Beth was getting into the car, I locked the front door. When I sat in the passenger seat, I handed Beth my key.

"What are you giving me this for?" as she stared down at the silver looking key in the palm of her hand.

"If something happens, I don't want them to have my house key, for obvious reasons. I'll knock on the door tonight and you can unlock it and let me in".

"Ok, I understand." Turning to face forward, while dropping my key into the centre console with her left hand. The index finger of her right hand, pushing the auto start button and the car fired up. We left the drive and headed into town.

# CHAPTER 11
## CASH

Beth pulled her car up onto the curb and over those two yellow painted lines, on the edge of where the roadside meets the concrete upstand of the curb line. I could see the entrance to the bank, standing out between the rows of charity shops, food banks and discount clothing stores. The green illuminated beacon, almost calling out to me. I turned to face Beth, just as the handbrake was put on.

"You'll get a ticket parking here" knowing fine well that she didn't care.

"I think a parking ticket is the least of our worries. Don't you think?" She tilted her head and smiled. She looked so joyful and at ease in that moment, her hair had become a little loose from when it was first tied up this morning and only accentuated her casual, yet pretty summer look. I returned a smile and leaned in to kiss her. Our lips connected for only a second. I thought this may be the last time I have that connection. As our lips parted, she spoke in a soft voice.

"Please be careful".

"I will be" and with that I left the car and waved her off. As she bumped down off the curb and drove towards home.

As I watched her car leave. I tapped my hands against my pockets, making sure for the hundredth time that I had my wallet and phone. Not only did I need to borrow money from Chris, but I also needed his help in getting my twenty grand out of my account today. Normally the bank is a little funny about big withdrawals and normally state that they don't have the funds available in the premises. Although I think that's just a line they spin to hold onto your money for a little longer.

As I walked along those lines of charity shops and food banks, I couldn't help but notice that a lot of people were waiting to enter the food bank and that was a saddening sight. I remember our family struggling to get by, but it was never like this. So many people trying to make ends meet and living day to day. It brought me back to an article I read in the Sunday paper. The very same morning I had discovered that Ben was dead, it said that statistically there are more food banks in the United Kingdom than there are McDonalds outlets. I don't know what statistics has got to do with it, either there is or there isn't, but that's what the article said.

Here they were, trying to feed their families and I'm heading to the bank to get twenty-five thousand pound to give to a stranger. Made even worse, by the fact that I'm giving it away for something I've not been involved in. These people need it more than him. But these people don't hold all the strings and the threat of violence.

I finally made it to the bank. As I walked in, I saw a well-groomed guy on reception. He clearly plucks his eyebrows, and no one gets that brown from the sun in this country.

"How may I help you today sir?"

"Hi, thanks. I'm here to see Chris Dobson" as I shifted, uneasy on my feet.

"That's Mr Chris Dobson sir" I guess Chris has gone power mad in this place, making everyone call him Mr "Not to me it's not, just tell him his friend is here to see him" the guy nodded and went off through the door directly behind him.

I found a seat and waited, scrolling on the BBC news channel on my phone. One of the headlines read,

"Police hold man in connection with the murder of Ben Stapleton". That must be Bibby, even DI Morrison told me they had picked him up. Before I could read any further down the article a voice shouted over.

"Mr Dobson will see you now, if you just head door the corridor and it's the last office on the left."

"I know where his office is but thank you." I should know where it is, he's been looking after my finances for years, helping me stockpile savings etc, and now I'm about to blow the lot. As I step through the door into Chris's office, I noticed the brass plague screwed on the outer side of the mahogany door slab, stating Mr C Dobson.

"Hi, Mr Dobson, is it?" as I tried to be jovial.

"Chris to you, but don't let the others in this place hear you call me by that" My suspicions had been correct, he has gone power drunk. As he sat behind his grand mahogany desk, in his tailored light grey suit.

"Anyway, sit down. What's all this about wanting to borrow money?" as his outstretched arm, with an open hand, signalled towards the vacant chair that was placed directly opposite him on the other side of his desk. I took the opportunity to sit in the leather-bound chair, turning from side to side. I had the whole speech planned in my head, but now I couldn't find the words that would escape my mouth.

"Come on man, you know you can talk to me". He was growing impatient.

Patience wasn't Chris's strong area of expertise, just ask the numerous guys with broken noses over the years for proof of that.

"Ok. I know about Beth getting the money out of our joint account and now I need to do the same with my personal account. I need it all out, and I need it all out today. But I'm still five grand short and I was hoping that I could borrow that from you?" I was straight to the point, just the way Chris liked it.

"She told you about your birthday present then?"

I sat and explained the whole situation to Chris. The only time he spoke, was when he phoned his secretary to cancel his meetings for the rest of the day. As I relayed the whole situation to him, not once did he seem uneasy or angry that I'd asked to borrow the money. Quite the opposite. He asked me if five grand was enough to keep me going until I got back on my feet again. Which was great to hear, and should things get any worse, at least I could always borrow more. Hopefully it wouldn't come to that.

"So now you know why I need the cash, can you help?"
"The five grand isn't an issue; I always keep my side cash

in the wall safe behind you" I turned to face the little black metal door that was embedded into the wall just above my head. I never noticed it when I came into the room. Then again, I don't normally scan rooms for wall safes, I leave that to the safe crackers to sort out. "Getting your money out, now that is the problem. I can make a few calls. Hopefully there is enough cash onsite to cover it" I guess the usual tale, of insufficient funds on the premises, is actually correct. As Chris bent down and retrieved a form from his top draw, he slid it over and asked me to fill it in. The form was to release my funds and leave a couple of hundred pounds in the account, for any outstanding direct debits etc. I filled it in and passed it over.

"Thanks, I'll get it sorted, one way or another, it's almost five o'clock. Meet me in the pub across the street. Oh, and I'm coming with you tonight" Thank God that he offered to come along. That's the one thing I hadn't yet asked of him.

"Ok I'll see you over there. And thanks Chris, you're a life saver" he just nodded, and I left the comfy leather chair and his office behind.

As I stepped back onto the cobbled street and the darkness of the bank, the sun was shining down. I headed to the nearest pub. This must be the one that Chris was referring to as it was the only one across the street and the only one

that looked decent enough for Mr Dobson. I pushed open
the glass door and the place was virtually empty, except
for a couple sitting in the window seats, enjoying some
pretty, decent looking burgers and a glass of white wine
set in front of the woman and a pint of beer in front of the
guy. Neither of them noticed my entrance and I wouldn't
blame them for it. As I approached the bar, there was a
pretty girl with brown hair standing behind it, not as
pretty a sight as Connors new victim Jade but still pretty.
She looked about twenty years old, wearing a black bib
over her white shirt and black trouser combination.

"Can I help you?" in her soft and delicate voice.

"Yes thanks. Could I get a bottle of beer please? One
of those on the bottom shelf in the fridge and put it on
Mr Dobsons tab" I went out on a limb. I had no cash on
me and didn't want to use my card in case it effected the
work that Chris was doing in the background.

"Of course, Sir. Will Mr Dobson be joining you?" I guessed
right. As flash as Chris is, it would only be right for him to
settle tabs at the end of the month and no need to carry
cash or card etc. His ego had stretched passed the doors of
the bank and even in here, they call him Mr Dobson.

"A little later yes" I replied as I collected my bottle and
found a quiet spot to enjoy it. Not that it was hard to

find as the place had an abundance of empty tables to choose from.

Once I picked a suitable seat. I took the first drink of my beer; it was cold and just what I needed right now. I placed the bottle in front of me on the table and waited for Chris. I pulled out my phone and sat scrolling the news again. As I read on further into the article about Ben. It said that the murder weapons had still not been found and were assumed to be in river where his body was found. I was interrupted again by a text message this time, and not Chris's lacky from the bank. It was from Connor.

"Got those phone recordings" I instantly replied, "Thanks mate, but not sure I'll need them now, I'll explain later" another text popped up.

"I've already emailed them over, no idea what's on them and I don't want to know, it's up to you if you choose to listen to them or delete them".

"Ok thanks mate" I replied. Another text from Connor, containing his signature thumbs up emoji.

As I put my phone away, Chris was walking through the door and heading to the bar. I was sitting far enough away that I couldn't hear what was said. But when he turned away and headed towards me, he was holding two more beers.

"What time are you dropping this off?" were the first words he spoke, as he pulled out a large envelope from his bag and placed it on the table.

"Six thirty, so you managed to get sorted then?" Knowing that the answer would be yes, as why else would he put on the show of producing the cash on the table.

"Yeah, no problem, I had to work some magic and ensure you had enough left in the bank so that it wouldn't look suspicious. But it's all good. It doesn't look like much, does it. When it's wrapped up like that?"

"No, it doesn't" I ran my hands over my eyes and let them fall to my side.

"So how is it going to work, we just both go and knock on Frankie's door and say, there you go?"

Chris had a point; I didn't know what to do. I did know one thing though, that Chris couldn't be with me when I dropped it off.

"I'm not sure, to be honest. But I do have to be alone, that doesn't mean you can't be there, waiting in the car.

But it must be just me with the money. That was the deal". As we sat there, and I'd now moved onto the second bottle of beer. It was getting close to six o'clock. We needed to start to get a move on, I don't want to be late when I hand over my life's savings.

"We better make tracks" I said to Chris, as he was draining the last drops of beer from his bottle, nodding in agreement as he was in mid swallow and couldn't speak, even if he wanted to.

As we got up from the table, Chris grabbed the envelope and stuffed it back into his bag. Walking from the bar, Chris turned and told the girl that he'd be in tomorrow night with some associates, and that they would need option one on the buffet service, whatever option one was, headed back into the sun light.

"Where is your car?" I said, when I was scanning the street.

"It's in the unground car park. Just wait here. I'll be two minutes" Chris left me standing on the side of the road while he went to retrieve his Porsche. I started thinking about the crime rate in this town, it maybe wasn't such a bad idea to park it in a secure place. If it was left on the street, it would either have key scratches, broken windows or worse, even stolen within about five minutes. The screeching noises woke me from my thought process, I couldn't see the car, but I could certainly hear it. And then in a second another tyre squeal and the green Porsche turned the corner and came into view. Pulling up in front of me, about two feet from the curb, I guess for all the money Chris has, paying for replacement allow wheels by daring to go too close to the pavement and scratching them was an expense he didn't want to incur.

Sitting in the Porsche was an experience in itself, it oozed luxury, while still maintaining a cool sporty motif. The leather seats and dashboard, lined with the same colour green thread as the paint work. And fancier still, by the air con cooled cup holders. Chris never drives slowly, and every car I've been in with, he drove like he stole the car and not owned it. As we left the centre of town and headed off towards Frankie's house.

"Look, when we get there, you need to park this around the corner. It's not exactly inconspicuous". Chris burst out laughing at that, and agreed to parking up, closer to Claires than Frankie's. That would give me a chance to walk around the corner and into, whatever I was heading into. Chris entered the estate and purposely went the long way around, avoiding the play park and Frankie's gaze, should he be looking out and waiting. As Chris pulled up, again, too far away from the curb. He reached behind his seat and grabbed the large envelope. Laying it on my knees.

"There you go, make it quick and if you're not back here in an hour I'm coming to find you!" I knew he meant what he said, especially when he reached behind his seat again, and produced a small baseball bat. He has never played baseball in his whole life and that thing was only ever going to get used to cause damage. Either to something or someone and knowing Chris, it was the latter option.

"Ok, I'm going, hopefully you won't need that" I looked down towards the bat and then stepped out of the car and closed the door. Chris wound down the window.

"One hour remember" as he tapped this finger against his watch face. No doubt an expensive watch too.

"Yes alright, I'll keep it quick" and turned to walk in the direction of Frankie's house, as I heard the electric window go back up behind me.

# CHAPTER 12
# DELIVERY SERVICE

I walked along the street, fumbling with the large envelope. Having the sudden realisation that I hadn't counted the money, to make sure that it was all there. Chris would have done that anyway. Counting money was his job and had been for the last twenty years. My heart was racing as I approached the corner, and with a final look back, Seeing my protection and back up sitting in his car, was a relief. I turned the corner, my vision slightly hindered by the over growing hedges on the boundary of the corner house. And then suddenly Frankie's house came into view and judging by the car parked outside, he wasn't alone, like I had hoped. I could see the black Range Rover parked outside, facing down the street towards me. No one was sitting in the front, so I assumed they were in the house and waiting for a payment from me. I got to Frankie's house and staring up the garden steps towards his front door I could see him through the front window, wearing a vest top and looking like the piece of shit that he is. He didn't notice me. This was my last chance to run and hide. But what good would that do, they would be around at Claires within the next ten minutes and get my home address, either by asking her or beating it out of her. Neither of those scenarios were good for me or her.

I headed up those garden steps and took one last deep breath, trying to stop my heart from beating right out of my chest and calm down, my clearly visible nervous state, before knocking on the front door. Bang, Bang, Bang. I stood and waited, looking, and slightly admiring, his lion head door knocker that I had just used. My mother's front door used to have the same thing, before Claire got a new uPVC one fitted a couple of years back. There was no answer. Bang, Bang, Bang. As the last knock fell against the wooden door, the handle and latch sounded, and the door swung open. "You're impatient, come in and go to the living room" as Frankie finally presented himself, in all his horrible glory.

I didn't say a word. I didn't need directions to his living room as it's the same house type as Claires and the one I grew up in. As I headed into the room, the suited guys were sitting on the sofa, and I headed to the single chair and began lowering myself into the seat.

"Who said you could sit down?" came from Frankie's lips as he was now standing in the doorway, making his way in

"Oh, I'm sorry" that was the first time I had dropped my guard, I didn't know if the suited gentlemen had noticed, but I certainly did. I couldn't play the hard guy role anymore, that was over the moment I had said the word sorry, and it was just a natural thing to say in any normal situation, but not here.

"I'm messing with you, just sit down we're all friends here" as Frankie burst into laughter. That was clearly a sign to show these guys that he was some hard nut. The suits never laughed and just stared at me, not saying a word.

As I lowered myself again, back into the seat now that I had Frankie's approval.

"I trust you didn't tell that faggot, cop friend of yours about this little visit" another show of power from Frankie. The two guys on the sofa turned towards Frankie and then towards me in unison, I could tell by the looks they were giving me, that my police friend was new information to them and unwelcome information to say the least.

"No Connor doesn't know about this" I addressed the room. It was the first time that I had seen the suited guys up close and personal. The tall slim one, was as I expected, clean shaven and almost suave. Sitting in his dark navy suit with brown brogues and a matching brown belt. The other guy was not what I expected. He had a shaved head, much broader than his friend. An ill-fitting suit. This guy looked more used to fighting in pub car parks than wearing this attire. And judging by the scars on his cheek and one above his eye. I was right.

"Good boy. Now, is that the money that you owe Tommy?" as Frankie's eyes went down from my face towards the envelope that I shoved down the side of me, wedged between my thigh and the arm of the chair.

"Yes, it is, it's all there, so what now?" I needed to get out of this place. It was well furnished and looked clean but had a smell of violence and I was becoming even more uneasy.

"Well, we'll need to count it first" I turned my head towards the opening between the living room and the dining room that was to my left. where the voice had come from. I only assumed that it was the four of us in the house. But as I turned, my eyes locked onto the new figure, and it was Tommy Carter. I had seen pictures of him in the paper before, and he always looked like a mountain of a man. But here he was, slim and small. Wearing a pristine, tailored, light grey suit. A gold chain hung from around his neck which held onto a gold cross that lay against his bare chest, where his shirt wasn't buttoned up to the collar. His hands ageing and covered in scars. The mark of where a ring used to sit. I could tell he didn't take that ring off very often, only noticeable by the tan lines it had left behind. His eyes held a gaze that struck fear into me. Eyes of a maniac, he looked like he could kill someone right now. but his voice was the opposite. Cool, calm and collected. not raised.

"Ok, count it, so we can be done" I was a little short with him, but I needed to get out of here.

"Ok Frankie you heard the boy, can you go and count it and let me know if he's paid in full" it wasn't a question that Tommy asked, it was an order. But Frankie answered him anyway.

"Yes boss" and Tommy responded with "Good lad", and he sat opposite me, on the other free single chair. We sat in silence. I tried to avert me eyes from Tommy, but he didn't spare me the same courtesy. His eyes never moved as they pierced into me. A shout sounded in the kitchen from Frankie and broke the awkwardness of the room.

"All here"

"Are we done now? and is that the end of it?" I asked directly into Tommy's eyes. But he didn't get the opportunity to answer, as Frankie came back into the room and stood in front of the fireplace.

"Did she tell you what the money was for?" a smug look crept across Frankie's ugly face.

"Yes, she did, now is this done?!" I could feel my blood boiling in that moment. And Frankie could see it too. He just raised his eyebrows and smiled right at me he wanted a rise out of me, and he was going the right way to get one.

Tommy spoke:

"We're done, but we have some insurance, should you decide to go and see your boy in blue friend".

"Insurance, what insurance?" Not only was I becoming angry, but I was also becoming confused by this whole situation. It was Frankie's turn to speak, as the bigger one of the two on the sofa stood up to stretch his legs. "Well, see. We had offered your wife the opportunity to pay the rest of her debt in kind. You know how good she looks, and you know that she can be a real slut too. We were all going to take turns on her. But she decided that your little cock would be enough, for now". I had heard enough of this shit from Frankie. My calm had gone, I looked up at Frankie, making sure I had his eye contact "You really are a cunt, aren't you?" No sooner had the words left my mouth, I felt the sharp sting and my head flew to the side, as the back of the big man's hand came flashing across my face with such force, that when it was done, I spat out a goblet of blood across Frankie's clean carpet. The big guy never said a word and I had no return.

"Now, now. I think you need to calm down, don't you?" My head was spinning, a mixture of emotions and pain. When Frankie had said that. I nodded in sorrowful acceptance.

"Or we might have to dress you up the same way as that whore wife of yours" I heard him speak and then I heard the paper hitting the coffee table in front of me. As I lifted my head slightly to follow the noise, I could see what he had meant. There must be twenty images, fanned out across the glass backdrop of the coffee table. All images of Beth, in various poses. Some in her white lace lingerie and some nude. Some of the pictures she had hands on her body, a man's hands, Frankie's hands, I could see the swallow tattoo on his right hand in the shot. I couldn't speak. But then Tommy spoke for me "Don't worry, it was only a bit of touching. This is our insurance. If you speak to the law about what's happened here today, then I won't stop my boys from going further with the beautiful Beth. You know what, I think she might like it too, not so sure that you would like it though, especially being tied up and made to watch. Oh, and obviously the pictures will go live, and I have contacts at the newspaper who would see to it that these were printed in the press. Do you understand where I'm going with this?" again his calm voice shining through, he has a special ability of being able to threaten someone with the worst outcome possible and still not raise his voice. I nodded to show that I understood, I couldn't find or think of any words. I also couldn't take my eyes of the images in front of me, my worst nightmare, being presented to me, by a group of criminals who intend to hurt my wife if I don't play by their rules.

"Good boy, you are free to leave now, and you won't hear from us again. That is unless you blab to your friend, then you'll be seeing a lot more of us. Pass him something to wipe the blood from his mouth. We can't send our guest home looking like that, what would people think of us?" Tommy was in full flow now. He knew he had me over a barrel, and he knew that this would never get back to the police. Two tissues landed on my lap as the big guy tapped me on the shoulder.

"Sorry about your lip." Those were the first words he had spoken since I came in here. I looked up at him and I genuinely believe that he meant his apology. I began wiping the blood that had ran from my mouth and down my chin. Tommy spoke.

"See, we aren't animals. Now get lost and give my love to Beth" he was an animal and an even bigger cunt than Frankie.

As I pulled myself up from the seat and headed towards the door, I looked back at the images on the coffee table. Frankie must have noticed me glance over at them "Don't worry about them, I'll make good use out of those later" and then came that fucking laugh again as he stood there and grabbed his crotch. I wanted to punch his nose through his brain, right there and then. But I'd be dead minutes after, and it wasn't worth the risk. I opened the door and didn't give Frankie the courtesy of a reply. I headed down the front step and threw my bloodied tissues onto his garden. I hurried out of the gate and walked fast down the street and round the corner, seeing the safety of Chris's car, in all its flamboyant glory and his smiling face looking at me through the front windscreen. I opened the door and got in.

"All sorted?" Chris said as my bottom landed against the leather seat.

"All sorted. Can you get me home now?" I needed to be home, and I needed to make sure that Beth was ok.

"Hey man, no need to tell the details, as long as it's done and that's the end of it" Chris knew when not to pry and I couldn't thank him enough for his silence right now. I grabbed my phone as Chris began my journey home. I wrote a text to Beth.

"All done, be home soon" and hit send, seconds later "Thank you, see you soon" was Beth's reply.

As Chris weaved through the street I couldn't get the images of Beth out of my mind, I needed to forget this. She was forced to do that photoshoot and you could see in those images that she wasn't enjoying what was happening.

"Almost home buddy" Chris broke the silence.

"Thanks Chris, and thanks for today" I'm very fortunate to have three close friends, that we would do anything for each other.

"Hey, no problem, I could use some excitement in my life. And don't worry about the five grand, it's a gift from me. God knows I owe you it anyway" Chris had point, I had been the one who gave him his deposit for his first house, so he could move out of his mother and father's place. His dad used to beat her and him and he was only starting out at the bank in those days and didn't have the cash or salary to afford his owe place. "Thanks man, but I couldn't do that".

"Well, I'm not taking it back off you" and a smile shot across his face. I responded with "We'll see" as Chris pulled up outside of my house, I leaned in and hugged him, I haven't done that in years. No words were exchanged in that moment. But he knew what he meant to me because of it. I unbuckled my seat belt and opened the door.

"See you on Saturday for the poker night".

"I wouldn't miss it" came back from Chris, as I closed the door and headed up my driveway. Chris's car sped off behind me and as I approach my front door, I could hear Beth unlocking it, she had taken my advice for once. The door swung open, and I collapsed into her arms and feeling her embrace. I kicked the door closed behind me, with the heel of my foot.

As we stayed in that hold in the hallway. I whispered into Beth's ear.

"No need to tell me the rest of what happened, Frankie had great pleasure in presenting the photos to me" she didn't speak for a moment, but I could hear her begin to cry, then see finally spoke.

"I'm so sorry, I didn't want to do it. But I had no choice"
"I know you didn't, that's how these types of people

work. But it's over now, and we can move on. It will take some time to get over this, but we will. We just need to be strong for each other and we also need to make sure that we carry on as normal. We can't let other people know what's been going on. That's the only way we'll be able to move forward".

She understood what I was saying as I was now looking into her teary eyes and leaned into her for a kiss. We held it there for a moment or two. When the kiss was broken, we decided to order some food to be delivered. Thank God Chris had left me with some cash in the bank. I get paid on Friday and that should help, ease the pain a little and we would need to cut back for a few months. But for tonight, pizzas and a couple of beers with my beautiful wife wouldn't hurt the bank too much.

After we ate in silence, and I started clearing the empty pizza boxes and empty beer bottles from the living room floor. I was contemplating telling Beth about what I had been thinking for the last few weeks. About how I'd thought she was having an affair and how jealous I'd been over her visits to her mothers' house and that I already kind of knew that even she couldn't put up with her mother that much. But I decided against it, we had both been through a lot these last couple of days. Well, it had been more like weeks than days for her and we just needed to move past this. So, I went on to discuss how she should continue her life as normal. For her to keep going to the gym, going out with friends. Especially the spa day on Saturday as I had my friends coming over anyway and we needed to keep up appearances. She was slightly hesitant at this, but ultimately agreed and that it would do us both good to have some fun and forget the whole thing or at least try to.

It was getting late and if I wanted to stick to my own rules of moving on as though nothing had happened, I needed to get some sleep and go into the office tomorrow. If for nothing else, just to catch up with Julie for a chat.

With that we headed to bed. Sleep easily came this time round, as I drifted off with my hand on Beth's thigh, not before telling her that I loved her first and her responding with the same words. I was tired and relieved that it was over, and my eye lids closed into golden slumber.

# CHAPTER 13
# BACK TO NORMALITY

After waking up from my deep sleep by Beth getting ready at the foot of the bed, for her morning gym session. I loved watching her get dressed on a morning, and especially into her gym clothes. Wearing those tight pants and sports top. More of a bra than a top, to be honest. But I never complain about my morning view. When she was ready, she leaned over my still half a sleep body and gave me a kiss.

"Good morning sweetie and now goodbye"

"Good morning, babe, have a good day and I'll see you tonight".

"Sorry, I'm heading to my mams tonight, I need to tell her that this is all sorted" she looked sorry as she spoke. Like she wanted to be with me tonight and not with the dragon lady but needs must.

"That's ok, I might go for a run then if you're not going to be here" I surprised myself when I said it. But I surprised

Beth even more, as she approached the bedroom door and turned with a shocked expression. "Go you. Have fun. Now I really need to go" I rolled over and tried to get a little more sleep, as her steps descended on the stairs, that jingle for her car keys noise echoed through the house, signalling that she'd reached the bottom. And the inevitable sound of the door slamming while its hinges clung on for dear life. Then she was gone for the day.

I managed to doze back off and only woke when my alarm went off on my phone, I can't remember the last time I had been awoken by that sound. Normally I'm up and almost ready before it goes off. I quickly got up and had shower. Holding my belly and saying out loud:

"You'll be gone soon".

I was determined to shift this weight. A little run tonight would be the start. When that first one is over and is out of the way and I get the feeling of enjoyment again, I'll be once again hooked on it. After getting dried I dressed in my Black suit and white shirt. I had originally picked out my navy suit, but it just didn't feel right and only reminded me of the previous evening and the slim silent guy on the sofa, which I didn't need. I headed for the front door, grabbing my laptop on my route out the house and towards my car.

Maybe, when we are once again, financially secure, I might treat myself to a new car. I've had this one for years and pulling into the director spot at work in this heap, wasn't great for my image in the office. Not that I cared about what those people thought of me at all. But I was starting to care about it myself.

I made it into work in good time. The roads seemed quieter this morning. Maybe it was that time again when the kids were off school and the morning drop offs weren't needed, so people could enjoy a traffic free morning for a change. Or at least for the next six weeks. As I pulled up, Julie's car was already there. She always beat me into the office. Even on days when I got in extra early to catch up on paperwork, she would still be sitting at her desk and waiting for me to make an appearance.

The usual welcome into the building occurred and I avoided any need to exchange pleasantries with most of them.

"Morning Julie" that was the only sincere good morning that was genuinely meant, and I'd said it about thirty times already in the one minute I'd been at work. "Morning boss, you feeling any better? Coffee is on your desk by the way".

"Thanks Julie, yes, much better" as I strode past her and into my cool empty office. I closed the door and got seated. I intended to make a real effort at any tasks that I had on the agenda for today and any that I missed yesterday. I set my laptop up and started scrolling through the hundreds of emails that I had in my inbox, marked as unread. How is it possible to accumulate so many in one day? I replied to most of them, in between taking slips of coffee and thinking Julie really is the best. Most of the emails were just general stuff really. Advice on how to approach a new client, some training requested and a brief scan of this month's numbers, again they were on the rise. Before I knew it, I had been catching up for an hour and a half. I was so engrossed in it that I hadn't even noticed that Julie had been into the office and re-filled my cup. When I finally did realise, I stopped and sent her a little thank you message on the internal chat thing that was built into everyone's computers. She sent a thumbs up.

When I was drawing close to the final thirty emails. So close to the finish line, I could taste it. I had seen the email from Connor, with a little attached icon next to it. I froze and didn't know what to do. I should delete it, that would be the sensible thing to do. I couldn't listen to them talking and I was petrified to hear them tell her to bring some lingerie with her when she dropped off the money the first time. I had managed to hold those thoughts out of my mind, for all of the previous evening and this morning. But now they had resurfaced and with a vengeance. I hovered over the delete button and contemplated my next move. I had an idea. Should something happen and those images became public. This would be my back up, she was forced, and I could pass it onto the police as evidence. I was aware that Connor is the police. But this was done underhandedly, and I wouldn't want to get him into any trouble over it in the future. I decided to file it away. Not deleted, but somewhere, some place where it wouldn't be a constant reminder of what had happened.

I managed to get all those emails cleared and had quite a productive day. Julie walked into the office as I was packing up for the day.

"I'm free for a drink tonight, if the offer still stands?" She looked a little different than normal, hair maybe, maybe her makeup was different. I couldn't place what it was.

"Sorry Julie, but I promised myself that I would go for a run tonight. I'll make it up to you. Next week we can, I promise" I felt bad, I could go for a run after a drink. A quick beer wouldn't hurt. But no, I had to get out and work these legs. One beer would turn into a couple and then when I get home, I'll just crash on the sofa and not bother to put my running trainers on.

"It's ok. Don't worry about it. I was free tonight that's all. No need to make promises" she was holding open the office door for me as I was leaving.

"Next week and I do promise" as I grabbed her hand. She let a little smile form on her face as her lips became slightly upturned.

"Bye, have a good night".

"Bye Julie, you too" as I headed to my car and pulled out of the car park. The journey home from the office wasn't as easy as my journey to it. I guess the schools aren't off this week and my traffic free morning was a fluke. I pulled up outside of the house, Beth's car was missing from the drive and then I realised that she was going to her mother's after work. I headed straight in and upstairs trying not to take too long or my motivation would dissipate. I quickly got changed into my shorts and my running top, which was feeling a little tight around my tummy area but that would soon fit me properly again over time. Providing I keep up with the running. I ran downstairs, I put on my old worn-out runner trainers and grabbed my headphones off the side, locked the front door and was playing around with the playlists while also trying to manoeuvre the earpieces to fit correctly and not fall out.

I decided to take my normal route, which was the same route that I'd walked home on Saturday night, the same night that Ben lost his life. It did feel a little strange to go on that route, given the circumstances. But I hated running around the streets and there would be less people to gawk at my sweaty mass along the riverbank. I walked for the first few hundred yards, as a little warm up, through a couple streets. Giving a hand up in the air hello to some of the neighbours that were either cutting they grass or just sitting on the front steps, getting the last of the sun, before it faded over the roof tops and onto the other side of the world.

I had reached the cut between the houses that leads down to the riverbank. I picked up the pace and pushed play on my phone, as AC/DC was just tuning up for Thunderstruck to play into my ear drums. I put my phone in the zip pocket of my shorts and concentrated on trying to keep my breathing steady. I hit the volume button on the earpiece to turn it up. One to drown out the sounds of my stomping feet and secondly to stop the noise from my rasping intakes of breath, which increased as I made my way along winding track, headed towards the little green bridge at Cox Green.

I was almost three quarters along the track, before I had to stop running and walk for a little while. I had managed to run for close to a mile without stopping and

I was proud of my achievement. Especially for a guy as unfit as I felt and looked.

After my breathing steadied out, I once again picked up the pace. Thin Lizzy now singing in my ear about a whiskey jar as the bridge was now in sight. Just a short way and once I had crossed over it, I planned to take another breather. I found that if I set myself objects or places to hit, it gave me a little goal to focus on. I had made it to the bridge and my calf muscles were beginning to burn, but I couldn't stop, I needed to make it across the metal platform before I would allow that to happen. The feeling of the sun on my back and the light breeze hitting my face, only served to remind me of just how much I enjoyed it and how much I was regretting not getting back to it sooner. My sore legs in the morning will remind me why I stopped in the first place.

I finally reached the other end of the bridge and collapsed down onto the stone bollard. Hands on my knees and bellowing plumes of hot breath through the air. I may have pushed myself too hard. My breathing was heavy, and the sweat was running from my forehead and into my eyes. I lifted the bottom of my t shirt to wipe the sweat away and give me back my eyesight. Turning to my left, I could see the Oddfellows pub only a hundred yards from me. Groups and couples, enjoying a night drinking in fading sun. I could murder a pint of ice-cold beer right now. But I need to continue. So, I turned away from the pub and started on my return journey. This time on the opposite riverbank, the side that Ben was found washed up on the side of. As I was progressing, my pace had slowed down, and I was taking more and more little breaks. Every little milestone I had set myself, I fell short of. Not able to keep up my earlier momentum. I had pushed myself too hard on the outbound journey and was really suffering now on the inbound.

As I stopped running once again and continued at brisk walking pace, I turned as the path followed in land slightly and to the car park. The same car park that me and Beth used to frequent in our younger days. The same car park that I had seen a car parked in on Saturday night, with its headlights shining. And now the same car park that was full of police cars and vans. With some guy in a suit talking into a camera about the ongoing search for the murder weapon. This was turning into a bit of a media frenzy. Nothing like this happens around here, and this is the main attraction right now. Some reporter getting his face on TV and no doubt a promotion to follow it, and this all came about, because a man with a wife and two kids has lost his life. There's some really fucked up irony hidden in there somewhere.

I tried to make my escape, unnoticed by starting to run over the grass and back towards the river. When I heard a shout "Sorry sir, but that footpath is closed for a police investigation" as I turned around and saying.

"Sorry officer, I'll go back the way I came" my eyes hit who that voice belonged to. It was Connor.

"Hey what's all this, you out running again?" as he grabbed a hold of my t shirt. It must have been a while since he's seen me exercise.

"Yeah, I just need to get rid of this mass" looking down at my tummy.

"Yeah, it'll do you good. I was talking to DI Morrison, and he said you'd given him a statement. I gave mine on Monday. I'm just helping him out a little here, keeping tubby guys from running along the riverbank, you know?" we both laughed at that. Then Connor went on. He lowered his voice for this part.

"Between you and me, they have Bibby tied up for this. He's confessed and said he dumped the knife along here. So that's what the search is for".

"Fuck me, why kill him, just for the sake of whatever he had in his wallet? It doesn't make any sense to me" it didn't make sense. Yes, Bibby was a small-time villain. But I never had him down for murdering someone. Connor corrected me.

"That's the thing, Ben wasn't robbed. They identified him by his driving license, and he still had about fifty pound in his wallet. Anyway, I'll have to get back. I'm on duty after all. See you on Saturday and I'm glad you managed to get sorted out with Beth, I hope you deleted the files I sent" as he tipped his cap towards me.

"Yeah, I did. See you Saturday. Thanks" as Connor walked off towards a group of other police officers, easily recognisable by their uniforms. I headed back in the direction I came from.

Heading back towards the metal bridge. I was sorry that Ben had lost his life. But by doing so, he had just increased my run from three miles to four. I picked up the pace, I had a long breather while talking to Connor and had now found a steady rhythm. My footfall landing in perfect unison to the base line of Queen and another one bites the dust. I never looked up further than six feet in front of me, trying to grind out the route home. My feet passed over gravel, dirt and then the metal of the bridge, for the second time. And still I didn't stop, I continued. My calves were on fire when I finally had to take break. I was now directly opposite the car park. Standing in the same spot that I had seen the car on Saturday night. Breathing heavy and exhausted. I decided to walk the rest of the way home. I couldn't bring myself to jog anymore. My legs would be hurting for the next few days from this. But I did enjoy it. It was great to be out and exercising again.

I finally made it back through the cut, leading into the housing estate. Passing the houses where only a short while ago, people were enjoying the sun. They were now enjoying their sofas as the sun had gone for the day. I turned into our street and Beth's car was on the driveway, it must have been a flying visit to her mother's house tonight as I hadn't expected her to be home yet. As I opened the door, I could hear her in the kitchen, rattling sounds coming from the room. And then the shout through the house "Just in the kitchen" confirmed her location.

"Just going in the shower" she didn't respond. I hope it's because she's busy making some dinner, I'm starving. Again, I hadn't eaten today and whatever energy I had left, was now gone from the exercise. After walking upstairs on my sore legs and peeling off my sweat drenched running gear I hopped under the water for the second time today.

I got sorted and just put on my customary house attire of shorts and a hoodie and headed downstairs where the smell of something delicious came wafting through the house. We sat and ate at the breakfast bar, while I told her about my day, and she told me about hers. In those hours of us just chatting and catching up, it felt like the good old days. Where we were one unit and not a divided force. Tonight, must be the first time in months that the TV in the living room wasn't turned on. Our whole night spent in each other's company was amazing. While Beth cleared up and loaded the dish washer, I grabbed my laptop and decided to put a half day holiday in for tomorrow. It was Friday anyway and nothing good happens on Friday afternoons. Plus, I needed to get shopping for supplies ready for Saturday and no doubt Beth would be interested in some retail therapy and maybe a new outfit for her spa day.

"You fancy going shopping with me tomorrow afternoon?" I asked over the top of my laptop.

"Sure, I finish at one tomorrow, so we could grab some lunch too. But can we go to bed now, I'm so tired?" I had to chuckle at that.

"Of course, we can" and for the second night running we went to bed at the same time.

# CHAPTER 14
## SHOPPING

I was sitting in my office just trying to count the clock down. Waiting for it to strike one, so that I could leave and meet Beth in town for some lunch and onto the shopping. I had a catch up with Julie, earlier in the day. I still felt a little bad that I couldn't go for that drink with her and we didn't have our usual chats yesterday, because I was too busy trying to catch up on the day I had off. We had a nice catch up. Just talking about how things were going at home and general stuff. Julie told me that Hannah, our dreaded HR manager had tried to put a meeting in my diary for this afternoon and Julie had blocked it as I wouldn't be here. She had conceded that a meeting with her on Monday morning would be acceptable. In Julies words:

"You can't hide from her forever, but it's Friday and no one needs to have her attitude ringing in their ears for the weekend" I could have kissed her for that. Julie and I always had the same understanding, I guess that's why we get on so well. She's a few years older than me and

I need her around to keep me grounded sometimes. But we have laugh in the office. Most times. Usually at someone else's expense. But what they don't hear, can't hurt them. Our catch up ended two hours ago, and I've been bored ever since she walked out and closed the door behind her. If it wasn't for the Regional Managing Director being onsite today, I would have left this place ages ago and started my weekend a lot sooner than expected.

It was now 12:50 and I figured that I would pack up for the day. I had the laptop bag over my shoulder as I passed Julie and spoke.

"See you on Monday, bright and early".

"Have a good weekend and I'll be in here before you get out of bed" was her response. She smiled and I smiled back, while nodding my head in agreement. Knowing fine well that she wasn't lying about any of it. I tapped on the Regional MD's glass office door and waved a hand at him, and he looked up over his numerous computer screens and I could only see the top of his head and his thick rimmed glasses. Then I headed down to the car.

I had agreed to meet up with Beth in the bar across the street from the bank. The one I'd been in only a couple of days ago to meet Chris. I had explained to Beth just how good the burgers looked and as we normally try and eat healthily at home, mainly due to Beth's strict gym regime and her keeping her toned body in check. But I thought we should treat ourselves and get a big fat burger each. Beth was going to take the bus in to town to meet me, as she didn't like to park her car in the multistorey car park. For fear that she would damage it, on those tight bends and tight parking spaces. As I entered the bar, I could see Beth sitting at the table, the same one I chose the day. Great minds do think alike. I held up my hand, in a way that looked like I was holding up a drink. She knew what I meant and used her own hand signals to make sure that I only ordered her a small one. I walked up to the bar and was greeted, again by the pretty girl in her black apron.

"Can I help you sir?" as she was straightening her clothes, after what looked like restocking the clear glass fridges underneath the spirit shelf.

"Yes, thanks. Can I have a bottle of that beer and a small white wine please? Oh, and a couple of menus too"

"Of course, sir" As she set down two menus on the bar in front of me and went over to the fridges to start my drinks order. As I stood and waited, I saw Dylan walking passed the window with his head staring down at his phone screen. I spun and held up two fingers to Beth and mouthed the word "Back in a second". I turned and headed back out of the bar, shouting towards the back of Dylan's figure as he continued his journey.

"Dylan, Dylan!" He spun round on the spot.

"Oh, hi mate. I'm just heading home, been ordering her (his wife) some jewellery for her birthday" as I caught up to him.

"Well, I hope you've got enough money to lose on Saturday night?" I can't remember the last time that Dylan had won at one of our poker nights. "Don't worry about that, my lucks got to change. Your place at seven?" Maybe his luck would change. He has been so down in the dumps lately and he could do with a lift.

"Yeah, seven should be fine. But Beth is out all day, so if you're bored you can always come round early, it'll be good to catch up" as I hit him in the arm. In a show of guy affection. Girl's hug and kiss each other's cheeks and guys hit each other.

"I'll see what happens. But I'll definitely be there" "Good man, ok I've got to go, can't leave the woman waiting. See you tomorrow" As I started to turn back towards the bar.

"Yeah, see you soon" I heard over my shoulder. I headed back into the bar and the pretty girl (I should really ask her name) had our drinks set out. She smiled as I approached her once more "Would you like me to put this on Mr Dobsons tab again sir?" in her soft voice.

"No, I'll pay on my card if that's ok" Thank God I got paid this morning or our date afternoon would have been spent sharing a packet of crisps at home. She didn't respond, she just held out the card machine, while I tapped the plastic against it.

I took our drinks over to the table where Beth was seated.

"Where did you go?" no hello honey, how was your morning, just that.

"Dylan walked by, so I went to see him".

"Oh ok, how is he?"

"Fine I think, he's coming over tomorrow. So, I'll catch up properly then. Anyway, enough about that. What are you ordering?"

"Well, I don't know, you haven't got the menus!" as the word left her mouth, I realised that I hadn't picked them up from the bar. As I turned and started to lift myself out of the chair, I saw the girl who served me heading over to see us, holding the two menu's I left behind. She placed them in front of us.

"You're a life saver" I said as she smiled and headed back to the bar.

After we sat and studied the menu. Well, Beth did. I already knew what I was ordering. The biggest burger in the house. We ordered and the food came out quickly, we only had to wait about fifteen minutes or so. I looked at Beth as I raised both my hands towards my lips. Hands that were filled with a seeded bun and between the bun was the juiciest double burger I'd ever seen. Taking that first bite and feeling the grease escape from the cooked meat felt amazing and tasted even better. The burger didn't last five minutes, and, in that time, I'd eaten all the chips that were scattered around the edge of the plate. Beth took a little longer to eat than I did, and her burger was half the size. But she seemed to enjoy it.

After the plates were cleared and Beth had finished her wine, it was now time to hit the shops. I only needed beer and some food for tomorrow night, but whenever I went shopping with her, it took hours and normally I hated it. But I was quite looking forward to seeing what new outfit she would pick out for her spa day. Well, she wouldn't be wearing much during the day as she'd be in the pool or sauna. But the outfit was for the meal that followed on the evening. We walked around a few clothing shops, with Beth constantly asking if we could afford for her to be splashing the cash on new clothes, given what's happened these last couple of days. I had to keep reminding her that I had been paid today and we needed to keep up appearances. Not just for other people's benefit, but also, for our own sake. We landed in the swimsuit section and Beth turned to me said.

"I think you should pick my swimsuit for Saturday. The girls will only see it once, but you'll get to see it a lot more" a cheeky smile crept across her face.

As I looked along the line of tiny bikinis and one-piece suits. My eyes landed on a white one. A little thing, more lingerie than swimsuit and the images of Beth lay on Frankie's bed, wearing only a white lace thong and his fucking hands pawing at her naked breasts, all came flooding into my mind. I must have frozen as these sick images passed through my mind, only broken from my internal nightmare by

"Are you ok?" as I turned towards her, I think the realisation of what I was thinking about had caught up to her, as her eyes went from staring into mine, over to the white bikini and then back at me.

"Maybe white isn't a good idea" she said, as I shook my head. "I think this is too soon" she said, while reaching out grabbing my hand.

"No, it isn't, let's keep looking" with her leading along the line and away from the white reminder, I saw a dark green one-piece swimsuit, low cut, and the front and when I lifted it off the rack, turning it around. I could see that it was high waisted, and I knew her butt would look amazing in this.

"Buy this one" I said, as I looked at her, still fighting to hold back the images that flashed through me. But I had to be brave and couldn't show Beth that it was affecting me so much. "Good choice Mr. but I'll need to get the right size. The gym hasn't taken that much weight off me" she giggled as she flicked through the items, finally locating her correct size.

After we had sorted out her daytime pool attire it was onto the dress and shoes. Obviously, she couldn't wear any of her fifty pairs of shoes that she currently owned. That would be madness. This was her expertise, and she was now on a mission to make sure that she looked the best out of all her friends. No doubt that every girl in the group was out there somewhere, trying to do the same thing, while also being followed around by their hapless partners. After going around a handful of shops,

I lost count of how many we had been in at this point and just followed her around like a little puppy. She finally settled on a short, dark red evening dress. Again, low cut. The dress would cling to her figure and show off all the hard work she'd been putting in at the gym. All this effort to impress her friends. She bought high heels in a matching red colour. The heel size made her close to my height and only served to make her legs look amazing. After we had both of her day and night outfits sorted, it was getting late.

"Can we go home now? I'm getting tired of walking around" as she looked over to me, while my hands were full of bags from three different shops.

"No, we can't, I need to get supplies for tomorrow night. That was the point of coming shopping in the first place" as I swung one of the bags to hit her leg. She just laughed and spoke.

"Ok, let's go and get your boys night crap then" as we headed off to the supermarket.

I stood next to Beth at the end of the till, as the most rude and slow checkout women rolled along our purchases to the sounds of beep, beep, beep. Beth made some sarcastic comment about, are you sure you have enough food. And I always reply with the same, we're growing lads, it won't go to waste. As the women pushed over the cheese selection, some nibbly bits and bobs and the cases of beer and the inevitable words came from her "Cash or card?"

"Card please" as I presented my card to the contactless machine. And we were all packed up and heading for home.

In the car Beth made another comment

"Do you think you have enough beer for the four of you? I mean will sixty bottles be enough?" I replied with "Maybe, well it will do for the first couple of hands, and I noticed that you didn't mention the three bottle of white wine that are all for you and not to be shared amongst your friends" She rolled her eyes at me. She was a black belt in eye rolling. It must be from all the practice she gets with me. Once we got home, Beth took the food stuff inside the house to put away and I loaded up the garage fridge with the beer. Filling it and still having a box spare, that I would have to reload, during tomorrow's poker game. When I went inside, Beth had put everything away and had changed into her PJ's, little shorts, and a loose-fitting t shirt. She had two glasses in between the fingers in one hand and a bottle of white in the other. A chilled one, which was always the case, as Beth liked to have a constant supply ready. Should any opportunity present itself.

"See. I do share with my friends" clinking the glasses together and sarcastic grin spread across her face.

"Ok, you win. I'll just get changed and we can have a relaxing night" when I returned downstairs and walked into the living room. Beth was texting someone.

"Who are you messaging now?"

"Oh, it's nothing, just the group chat and sorting out for tomorrow" while she sipped delicately at the large wine glass, savouring it for all its glory. Seeing her with her phone only reminded me about the recordings I had hidden away on my laptop. It would be so easy to grab it from the bottom of the stairs and just listen to whatever was hiding there. But I couldn't. At least not now I couldn't. I decided in that moment, that I would listen to the tapes at some point, as I just needed to get it out of the way and then it would be done. And with some luck, I can put that part behind me at least. But not tonight. Tonight, I was going to vegetate in front of the TV, drinking nice wine, with my wife sat next to me.

As the hours rolled by and the wine flowed. This would normally be the time, when Beth became a little more flirtatious or arms being touched. Generally, the signal that the night wasn't over, but it was extended to the bedroom instead. But tonight, was different. She remained on her side of the sofa. Reaching her legs over to my side and resting her feet on top of my upper thighs. That was the most I had touched her tonight. After the ordeal that she had been through at Frankie's house, I wouldn't blame her if she never got in the mood again. I can't begin to comprehend what must have been going through her mind that night. Not knowing if they would stop and not knowing what would come next. The images again, circling my mind. As clear as the moment Frankie had dropped them onto that coffee table for them to burn a constant reminder into my retinas. I looked over at Beth, trying to see her in a different light. And not the one in my thoughts. She had fallen asleep with her empty glass in hand. She looked so innocent and comfortable. Maybe this was the perfect time to listen to those recordings, but those can wait. What's important right now, is that I take care of her.

I got up and started doing the usual house locking up routine, prised her glass from her sleeping fingers and loaded up the dish washer. Went on to lock up the doors and turn off various light's downstairs, while she slept. When it was time for bed, I thought about waking her. But she hadn't found sleep too much these last few days. So, I leaned over and hooked my arms under her light frame. I bent my knees and used my legs to push me up, holding her in my arms to carry her upstairs. Her eyes opened slightly, only for a second and then they were closed again. Her arms were awake though, as they reached up and wrapped around my neck as I carried her upstairs to our soft bed, for her to sleep like an angel.

# CHAPTER 15
# POKER NIGHT

"How did I get here?" Came her voice in my ear, as I was lay in bed playing on my phone. I hadn't wanted to get up and risk disturbing her from that golden slumber that had been evading her for days. Even though I was in desperate need to use the toilet.

"You fell asleep on the sofa, and I carried you up to bed" not moving my eyes from my phone screen as I spoke. "I just remember watching the end of that movie, the one with the girl in the yellow tracksuit and she swings the sword around" I laughed at that, movie titles were not Beth's forte.

"Yeah, when I looked over you had dozed off, when the credits started" she snuggled into me, and we lay there for as long as I could hold my bladder.

Our morning was uneventful, Beth catching some sun in the garden, and I walked up and down the lawn, following my petrol mower. And I tidied up the borders and de weeded them, just like Beth's father had taught me. While she still just lay there, until she had to start getting ready. I had agreed to drop her off at the spa and she would grab a taxi home much later.

When she had finished getting ready and walked out into the sunshine once more. Wearing a wraparound skirt and the green of her new swimsuit covering the top half of her body. I instantly regretted picking that one out. She looked amazing. So sexy that I prayed both our cars had broken through the night, so she had to stay with me.

"What do you think?" as she twirled on the patio in front of my gawking eyes.

"You look amazing".

"Aw thanks, I thought it would be easier to wear this to travel there in, just saves time getting changed. Plus, it's less to carry. See, always thinking". While tapping her finger against her temple. I had to admire her idea. It's the same thing me and Dylan used to do as kids. Wear our swim shorts under our clothes, so you didn't waste any valuable pool time.

"Do you want dropping off now?"

"Yes please. And can I have some money too?"

"Yeah, I reached into my pocket and passed her my bank card.

"Just use that one, I won't need it until tomorrow anyway" Having passed over my card, we headed out. I decided to take Beth's car. As it was much better than mine and she probably wouldn't appreciate being dropped at the entrance of the fancy hotel in my heap of a motor.

When we got there. I gave her a kiss and told her to enjoy herself. She picked up her bag from the footwell. It had her red dress and new heels hidden inside. She closed the door, and I left her there. The guys would be coming over in a couple of hours and I need to get the place sorted. I put my foot down in the Mercedes and the miles home flew over. I do need to treat myself to something like this. But I just can't afford it anytime soon. Once I arrived home. I took a quick shower and got changed into some jeans and a white t shirt and started to get prepared for tonight's event.

I laid out the foldable poker table cover across the white granite of the breakfast bar and set the four stools out, so that we would be close enough to the cloth but leaving enough space between, that we wouldn't be able to see each other's cards. That way, no one could accuse another of cheating. Once the setting was right, I placed two decks of cards on top and started counting out the chips and made sure everyone had the same amount. The game was only twenty pound each, but it was played seriously. Obviously with the banter between us, flowing over the top of the cards.

Great, everything at the table was set. Now to start on the food. A quick glance at my watch and it was now getting close to 6:00pm, so I had an hour to prepare the rest. I started by emptying out some crisps into bowls and lining up the dips to accompany them. Then some little nibble on the plates. Just sausage rolls and some chicken pieces, all were precooked, as I couldn't be bothered with the hassle of stopping the game, to switch the oven on when people got hungry. After placing these on the edge of the kitchen countertop, the part that faces towards the breakfast bar, the front doorbell rang. Saying out loud to the empty room "Very early" as I walked through to the front door, opening it. I saw a small boy maybe only seven or eight years old, standing there holding his football. I looked over the top of him and a woman was standing at the end of my drive.

"Go on then!" she shouted at the boy.

"I'm so sorry Mr but I kicked my ball off your car. It isn't hurt. I promise" clearly his mother had made him apologise.

"That's ok kid" and shouting over the top of the boy's head. I said "and thank you" to his mother, or at least I assumed it was his mother. As the boy turned and walked back down the driveway. I remembered my mother making me do the exact same thing at Mr Jones's house. But I deserved that, as my football had smashed his living room window.

When I had closed the door, I could see my laptop bag staring up at me from its resting place at the bottom of the stairs, begging for me to open it up and listen in on my wife's conversions. I shook my head, an attempt to shake the thoughts from my brain and turned to get back to the food. I opened the drawer and took out my favourite knife. Whenever I cooked, I always use this to chop everything. It's not ideal for cutting through cheese, turning blocks into slices. But it cost me a fortune and I intended to get my money's worth. I worked through the various types in front of me. Mature cheddar, some stilton and then some brie. I placed the knife down and started laying the slices across the wooden serving board, that Beth made us buy, for when we had guests round for fancy food. I opened the packet of crackers and spread them evenly around the cheese selection. I just had just enough will power to stop me from eating some of the delicious food in front of me. When the doorbell rang again, I looked down at my watch and it was close to seven o'clock. I put the knife on the side and went to open the door.

When I opened the front door, I was greeted by my three best friends. They must have arranged to share a taxi. No doubt, Chris had arranged it and picked up the other two on route as he lived the furthest away.

Dylan was the first one through the front door. It was the first time in months that I hadn't seen him in his work clothes. I almost forgot he owned normally clothing. Then Connor followed him in, dressed smart and carrying a box of some exotic beer. He always had an acquired taste. And lastly through the door came Chris, who was looking out towards my car.

"I see she didn't get you the new car yet?" Knowing fine well, that the money was never intended on such a lavish birthday gift and that was his way of subtle humour. I didn't like his comment one bit. But I played along with it, for the sake of the others.

"No not yet, I'll have to have words with her" We both laughed. His at my expense and my laugh was a fake. We all headed into the kitchen.

"Take a seat chaps. I didn't think you'd be here this early. Help yourselves to the food. I need to get the beer out of the fridge in the garage" as Dylan and Chris walked around the breakfast bar, now turned into a poker table for the evening. Connor spoke.

"I'll give you hand" with that, me and Connor headed out to the garage, while Chris and Dylan were chatting.

I was passing out the cold bottles into his outstretched hands, Connor said.

"Listen. I have something I need to tell you".

"Sure, what is it?" as I turned back and forth from the open fridge.

"Well, when I got those recordings for you, I had to tell the guy that it was in relation to a case I was investigating. A case that involved Frankie Jackson. Well now the guy is listening to the tapes, because of voice recognition, Frankie's voice is on those recordings. I don't know what she's been up to. But I thought you should know that she might get caught up in the case"

"Shit. I never wanted that. I haven't even listened to them yet. Anyway, can you stop him?" as I closed the fridge door, while Connor stood there with his arms full of beer.

"I only got the call twenty minutes ago. Out of courtesy. I'm not high enough up the food chain to stop the process. He's listening to them now. But hey, I mean, she isn't a stupid girl, who'd be mixed up in drugs and it's maybe just something innocent. You know" that was Connors way of trying to make me feel better. He was right she wasn't mixed up in drugs, just mixed up with debt and Frankie's sordid images of her.

"Keep me in loop mate, I want to know if she is in trouble" I lied to Connor, I knew what the issue was and why his voice was recognised on those calls. But I couldn't bring myself to tell him the truth, at least not yet. "Come, let's get drunk and lose some money" Connor said as we left the garage and headed into the house.

As Chris and Dylan had taken the stools on the outer side of the poker set up, me and Connor took the stools that had our backs towards the kitchen.

"Let's play" Chris said as he picked one of the two decks and started dealing. We played a few hands as we had a couple of drinks. Connor told us all about Bibby confessing to killing Ben and that they had managed to find the murder weapon, which was a kitchen knife. According to Connor, it had Bibby's prints all over it. And some other prints that were still to be confirmed. But given Bibby lived with his mother and sister, it would probably be one of theirs. Chris had to join in, explaining to everyone that he always hated Bibby and we all knew why. Dylan looked a little rough and with some gentle persuasion from Chris and Connor, he finally let it slip that he'd just had a big bust up with his wife over money, and the fact that he was coming around here tonight. I could tell something was bothering him, from the moment he walked in. He had sunk quite a few more beers than the rest of us.

I won a few hands and so did Chris. We were all having a good time. Even Dylan managed to feel a bit more jovial, especially when Connor was telling him about his new girl, the lovely Jade. And how much younger she was than him. That's when Chris called him a cradle snatcher and a lucky bastard. I spat beer across at Dylan when I heard that. Which only made us laugh some more. We had a little break to get some of the food eaten and then cracked back on with the game. Dylan had won a couple of hands, but his chips were still pretty low. I contemplated throwing a couple of hands, just that he would win. But decided against it because Chris would smell a rat and would know what I was up to. I was trying to take my time with the drinking, as the other three were knocking them back, I wanted to keep my wits about me and win this game at the end. I checked my watch it was nearing ten o'clock. Dylan was raising the stakes with what little chips he had in front of him. He must have a good hand. Chris decided to call his bluff and bet just enough, that if Dylan wanted to see out this hand, he had to go all in. Dylan drained another bottle of beer and slid all his chips into the middle of the poker table. Me and Connor had already folded at this point and Chris said.

"Ok, so what you got?" as Dylan turned the two cards in front of him over. He held a pocket pair of nines and along with the two aces in the middle of the table, that gave him two pairs. Not the best hand, but certainly worthy of going all in. Chris smiled as he turned his two cards over. An ace and a jack. Chris had three aces and Dylan was now out of the game completely.

"Fuck!" shouted Dylan.

"Better luck next time my friend" came from Chris's lips as he slid the huge amount of chips from the middle of the table, over towards his already ample pile. With Dylan now out, I decided it was a good point to take another break for people to use the toilet and top up drinks etc. It would also, give me the opportunity to check in on Beth, who I hadn't heard from since I dropped her off at the entrance to the hotel. I grabbed my phone and quickly texted.

"How's it going babe?" a few minutes passed, and a reply came back "So good, I'm very relaxed and having a good catch up, I'll be home at around 11:30 and I'll see you then".

"Great. See you soon" I hit send and dropped my phone back onto the table.

We all sat back down on the stools to get this game over with, except Dylan, who was standing up and asked if he could crash on the sofa for tonight, as he was a little drunk and couldn't be bothered with the wife having another go at him. I said that was fine and that there were some throws in the basket, by the side of the sofa if he got cold. He nodded and headed off into the living room.

"Guess he's done for the night?" Chris said.

"Yeah, he looks hammered" as Connor joined in. "He'll be fine, now can we get this game over with. Your taxi's picking you up at 11:15 right?" I was addressing them both. Chris added.

"Yeah, it is, but Connor wants to walk home".

"Not to my house though, to Jades" as the cheeky smile spread across his face. With Dylan now out and the stakes on the up, it didn't take that long for Connor to be next out. With me left fighting for dear life with a small amount of chips and Chris holding the monopoly over me, a few bad hands and Chris had taken the lot. He had the bragging rights for the next couple of weeks and our money too.

It was getting towards the time for them to leave. They both stood up and half attempted to help me clear away the mess. Boxes of empty bottles were laid on the floor next to the patio doors and all the plates of half-eaten food were cleared into the bin and then loaded in the dish washer. I folded up the poker tabletop while they stood in the kitchen finishing their last drops of beer from their bottles. It was quite nice to see the white granite top of the breakfast bar again. I looked over at them, and Chris had his head in his phone.

"Taxi's here" We said our goodbyes and I walked them to the door. Chris went straight to the taxi, waving a hand in the air as he strode down the drive. Connor turned and spoke to me.

"I'll let you know what's going on about those recordings ok" and put up a thumb as a signal that it would be nothing to worry about. Then he was off too. As I closed the door, I spotted my laptop bag. Again, it was screaming at me to listen to the phone calls.

"Oh, Fuck it" escaped me to the empty hallway. I grabbed the bag and headed towards the kitchen. I popped my head into the living room and match of the day was playing on the TV to itself as Dylan was lay across the sofa with his eyes closed. Poor guy would rather sleep on a sofa than go home to his wife. I continued through to the kitchen and sitting on the stool that I had been all night. As my laptop was loading up, I grabbed my work headphones from the bag, as I didn't want whatever was on the tapes to be heard by Dylan, if he woke up. I doubt he'll be awake until the morning, but I didn't want to take the chance. I scrolled through my emails, then realised I'd saved it in the separate folder. There it was. The email from Connor. Shouting out to me, begging to be opened. The text was just a blur to me, as my eyes were burning and fixated onto the attachment, labelled 'Private telecommunication records'. My heart was thumping as I opened the attachment. And there it was. A full list of every phone call my wife had made in the month.

I recognised my number from the last four digits. I could never remember my own number, let alone anyone else's, but that was mine alright. It featured a lot less than another number that was either phoned or received pretty much daily. I could have picked anyone of those hidden conversations. But I knew which one I needed to listen to. The one that Beth told me didn't happen. The one that I was sure I had heard in my drunken state from the other side of our bedroom door last Saturday night. The one that had a time stamp of 12:23.

I turned up the volume on my laptop and clicked play on the 30 seconds of recording. With the first voice sounding out into my ear drums. I didn't hear the front door slam this time.

# CHAPTER 16
# TRUTH

The words played through my headphones and directly into my brain. The recording wasn't the best of quality. Very similar to the old pirate VHS videos that me and Claire would watch as kids, sitting in front of the TV on Saturday mornings, watching Jurassic Park or Dumb and Dumber, while Mam and Dad were still sleeping upstairs. Or at least that's what they used to tell us they were doing.

One of the phones must have been dropping in and out of signal as the voices had a crackle to them. But I could make out Beth's voice, whether I recognised it through the crackling or just knew that it was her. I couldn't be sure. It had to be her, it was her phone and her phone records that had been sort for me via Connor. The male voice in the conversation was familiar, but with the quality not great, I couldn't place exactly who it was. It must be either Frankie or Tommy, even one of his two sidekicks maybe. I must have been one of those two who held the camera, while Beth stripped for them all and Frankie had a good grope of her naked body.

My guess would be that the slim guy held the camera that night. There was something about that guy, he never said a word the other day, but he has a look of the perverse about him.

A figure passed by my side, as I stared intently at the screen, watching the time on the recording ticking down slowly, almost in slow motion. I only realised that someone was there when a shadow cast across the laptop screen. Caused by the cascading light from the spotlights we had fitted in the kitchen/dining room, hitting against the person's silhouette. A gentle hand landing on my shoulder and a bag dropped onto the breakfast bar over the top of my screen. Still, I didn't look away from the screen. The time along the bottom reading fifteen seconds played and another fifteen still to go. The red of her dress catching my peripheral vision as it flowed past me and around the breakfast bar. Even with the crackling of the recording I could hear every word between them spoken.

I sat there, listening to the last part, the part that was spoken while I was stood outside of our bedroom door last Saturday night, trying to make out what was going on behind it. My shoulders, where Beth had only a few seconds ago, placed her soft hand had now sunken down, like a boy being told off by his parents. Intakes of breath becoming harder and harder. I couldn't understand what was happening. Was it rage building inside me? Or was it sorrow, sorrow for a life I was wasting?

The timer along the bottom of the screen had reached the end of its path. And I sat there in silence. Considering my next move. I could see her body moving, arms waving, trying to attract my attention. It worked, I broke from my daze and finally lifted my head up to look at her for the first time since I had dropped her off earlier today. I watched her mouth moving, her lips opening and closing, and the silence continued. Again, her mouth moved, this time I could see what she was saying, but couldn't hear the sounds, as she mouthed the words.

"Is everything ok?". My eyes fixated upon her own. Eyes that I loved. A tear formed in the corner of my own eyes as her mouth repeated the question over, and over again "Is everything ok? Is everything ok?" I took a deep breath and pulled the headphones free from my ears, going from silence to the loud voice emitting from Beth. Once more came those words.

"Is everything ok?" This time I heard her. As I screamed from deep within my lungs

"IS EVERTHING FUCKING OK! SHUT UP AND LISTEN!" That is the first time in our twenty years together that I have ever raised my voice in anger towards her. The frightened expression on her face and her backwards steps that she took showed me that she didn't like this side of me. She was scared of me in that moment. I could see the fear in her eyes. The man who vowed to take care of her all those years ago, was now a man she feared. I remained seated on the stool, as I hit the play button again on the recording. This time pulling out the headphone wire from my laptop, so that the recording would play out loud to the room for us both to enjoy. I didn't notice my phone lighting up from an incoming call, placed at the side of my laptop as the first voice spoke.

"Hi is it over?" Beth's voice sounded upset on the call, like whatever it was she was asking, she didn't really want to know the answer. I never shifted my gaze from her eyes, you could see the sudden realisation, deep within those eyes, that she knew where this playlist was going. "I got the call from Tommy to say that it was all sorted" the recognisable, if not miss placed voice replied. Beth interrupted him in mid flow, clearly anxious for an answer "So it's done?"

"No, it isn't, I got a picture sent to me, while Tommy was on the phone. He was still in the pub, you sure he had the green coat on?"

"Yes, I'm sure, I made sure he remembered to wear it. If it's not him, who the fuck did he kill?! Shit I think he's home now. What have we DONE... IT'S cost twenty-five grand so far and they've killed the WRONG man, I have to go" and the recording was over. Beth was leaning against the wall, facing me over the top of the breakfast bar, I couldn't stand up. Between her tears and historical mumblings, I could only make a few words of

"I'm sorry" repeated over, and over again. I placed both hands on the countertop and just before I attempted to lift myself from the stool. Her hysterics stopped and her face changed. Still the tears rolled from her cheeks, but she had something else on her mind now, her face was expression less and for the first time her eyes shifted from mine. Looking up above my head and then she screamed "NO STOP!"

The slight sting came from my shoulder blade. One second it was there and then it was gone. Moving towards my chest, piercing through me. I looked down at my right breast plate and could see the point poking through my t shirt. I blinked and when my eyes opened again, the point was gone. Now being replaced by a dark red circle, a circle that continued to grow. Just like throwing a stone into a lake and watching intently as the ripples coursed out, until they reached the outside of the lake and died at the grass verges. I couldn't think straight. My mind overflowing with everything. But one certainty that did stick, was that I had just been stabbed and I would no doubt be stabbed again if I didn't stand up and try to fight. I took the deepest breath I could, I could hear the internal bubbling of blood, as my breath was now escaping me from my wound. With all my strength I lifted myself up, looking at Beth, she had her hand over her mouth to stem her screams. Some from fear and some from the unknown. My head screaming at me. "Get on your feet, get on your feet, get on your feet". As I reached a standing position, I could hear the stool fall and hit against the tiled kitchen floor. "Turn around, turn around, turn around before the knife goes in again" was I could think of. I followed my minds order and as I spun, the knife struck again, this time hitting my stomach. I gripped the hand that held it, trying to stop it going in any deeper. Looking at my white knuckles, they looked like I was clinging onto a cliff edge, for dear life. The knife that had pierced my lung and was now jammed into my stomach. It was the same knife that I sliced the cheese with earlier tonight.

Still looking down at the handle, that same red circle now appearing. My white knuckles now splatted with blood that had dripped from my open mouth. I found the courage to draw out the knife from my belly using whatever strength I had left; I needed to lift my head and look into the eyes of my killer. Lifting my chin from my chest, between coughs of blood and the pain shooting through my upper body, the deep red circle ever growing across my torso. I made it to the face of the man who wanted me dead. As my blood ran down my chin I spoke in a rasping voice, unable to take a full breath and a mouth full of blood. The only word that would come out of my shocked and now pierced body was "DYLAN".

The look in his eyes were filled with anger and resentment. Burning red, like those old horror movie monsters. I saw Dylan as one of those monsters now. A monster coming to take my life. What had I done to him in the past, that I deserved to die at his hands. I love that man staring back at me, I needed to get some control, I needed to fight, I needed to live. If I was ever going to get out of this situation still breathing and keep my promise to little James about our park adventures. Keeping one hand tightly gripped on his, the hand covered in my blood that held the knife. I raised my free hand, clinched a tight fist, and threw my hand through the air. My blow struck his white flesh catching him in the centre of his nose. I read somewhere that it can disorient people, if done right. I had done it right, his eyes blinking in quick succession. His nose started to pour blood from his nostrils, running over his open mouth and gritted teeth, I bought myself a few seconds. I heard steps behind me. I spun around still holding on to his knife hand, this helped me keep my balance, my eyes spotted Beth as she was quickly approaching with her arms stretched out in front of her.

She was obviously going to attempt to hold me and let Dylan finish the job. I swung the back of my free hand in her direction, feeling my knuckles connect with her. Catching her on the side of her face, somewhere between her cheek and eye socket. The smacking sound was loud. As were her screams of agony. With her being of slight figure, the backhand sent her sliding across the floor, in a pile of tears and the red fabric of her dress. I could see the back of her head lifting from the floor and then it crashed down again, and she didn't move. I returned to face Dylan, still gripping his hand tightly, my second blow from my clinched fist towards his direction, again, connected with his face. Not on his nose this time, I aimed a little lower, cutting his upper lip. And the third blow came straight after. As the hit landed, again on his nose, this time. I heard the crack of his cartilage breaking. My rage was at a high and I could just about keep my balance, I'm losing a lot of blood here, and this fight can't go on for long. He still held onto the knife. As I raised my hand once more. I had forgot about Beth, being behind me. I was quickly reminded of her presence when my laptop cable was wrapped around my neck and drawn in tightly. I could feel it cutting into my throat. I thought I'd knocked her unconscious; how wrong I was.

She had a fight in her and now it's her time to show it. My breaths coming in short bursts now. I held onto his knife welding hand, for as long as I could, before my body began to give up and I fell to my knees. I let go of his hand and raised both hands to my throat, in an attempt to free my neck of the wire now cutting deep into my flesh. I need to breathe. My vision is becoming blurred as the blood was trapped in my head. As Dylan stepped closer to me, I could hear my name being called for. "Jonny, Jonny, Jonny" followed by banging sounds. The voices were fading as my breath left me. Then the knife struck again and again. Unable to fight any longer, the wire became loose around my neck and a fell to the ground, like a tree being felled in the forest. The side of my face hitting the cold tiles and another cough erupting from me, sent blood across the tiled floor. The voices continued, "Jonny, Jonny, open up" again, followed by the thud of bangs.

I could feel hands on my body, gripping my t shirt and tugging and wrenching at me as I was rolled onto my back. Through blurred vision and the fading pain, I looked up towards the ceiling light and there were the two figures glaring down at me of Beth and Dylan. Beth's dress was torn at the shoulder and her right eye now swelled and a small amount of blood ran from her cheek. Dylan was holding his nose to stem his own bleeding with one hand and still gripping the knife in the other. The knife held up in front of me, now blocking the light bulb from my sight. It came down and sunk into my chest again, from Dylan's cold hand. I could hear the point of the blade, scraping on the tiles underneath me. The blade had gone right through my body with ease. Beth was stamping and kicking into my ribs. With every fall of her foot and when it connected to my bloodied body, a burst of blood came from my lips.

This is the end of my life. Ended by the two people I loved most in this world. My best friend hadn't given a second thought to plunging the knife in again. I could see the blade rise and fall into me multiple times, I don't know how many, but it was enough for me to stop breathing. As my eyes began to close the red sole of Beth's heels came down upon my face. Those voices again "Jonny, Jonny, Jonny" the bangs of splinting wood followed. Then a huge crashing sound. As shouting and screaming erupted within the room, my eyes opened only momentarily and then they closed for the last time. I lay there on the floor feeling cold from the tiles and being drained of my life source. The pain had gone. I'm done with this world.

# CHAPTER 17
# CONNOR – HEADING HOME

Jonny's front door closed behind me, and I headed down the driveway, as Chris left in the taxi. Watching the red lights on the back of the car disappearing down the street. The taxi turning the corner at the bottom and then they were gone. I shouldn't have drunk so much, I can't imagine Jade will be too pleased when I turn up at hers and crash on the sofa, unable to perform in the bedroom. I need to freshen up, hopefully the walk to her house will help with that. I grabbed my phone from my pocket and text Jade,

"I'm on my way" as I took a few more unsteady steps, still holding my phone. A reply came back.

"Can you come to the pub? Aunty Gill left early, and I need to lock up" I replied back, concentrating on my text, to make sure I didn't make any spelling mistakes "Yeah, should be there in about 20 mins".

As I reach the corner of Jonny's Street, I didn't follow the same route that Chris's taxi took, I turned left and just made it across the road before another speeding cab turned into the street. That must be Beth on her way home. I could see a girl in the back seat of the taxi, but that could have been anyone really. But the estate was more catered towards the older generation and late-night taxis wouldn't be a common occurrence so it must be her. I headed down towards Fatfield bridge. A walk along the river would do me good. I know it's where Ben was killed, exactly a week ago to the day. But that was the side of the river that had some lighting along the path. Crossing the bridge, I looked over the edge to my left. The tide must be coming in, as the water was flowing towards me upstream from the mouth of the river at Roker/Hendon, depending which side of it you stood. Twigs and litter that were washed along the river, were now banked up on the sides. In daylight and when the riverbank verges had been cleaned, this spot I was standing in right now, had to be one of the most picturesque places in the northeast.

I continued on my way, turning a sharp left, and headed along the river's edge. Another hundred or so yards and I would make it to where Ben's body was found, and the area that was swept for any evidence, ultimately finding the murder weapon, and almost certainly leaving Bibby in prison for a lot of years to come.

The pathway now reopened to the public and no blue and white police tape in sight. It was almost as if nothing had happened here. A single bunch of flowers tied off to a tree was the only reminder that a life was lost at this spot, such a short time ago. As my feet kept moving and my eyes fixated upon those flowers, now starting to wilt from not being watered for a week. I tripped on a fallen branch, sending me into a forward stumble. Trying to remain on my feet was virtually impossible, my centre of gravity was off, my head leaning forward, and my legs scampering to try and catch it up. I went off the path and my legs gave up on me. Landing in a mixture of high uncut grass, brambles, and a few nettles, just for good measure. I wasn't hurt, thankfully. But I couldn't stop laughing, more from embarrassment. I was glad it was late, and no one was around to see that. If someone had showed me a fall like that, I would have shared it with everyone. As I was bringing myself back to my feet and sweeping off the grass that now clung to my legs, as a reminder of what just happened. I saw a shimmer in the now flattened foliage from where my body had landed.

I ran my fingers through the weeds to try and retrieve whatever it was. It was probably just a beer bottle top, from some kids having a little underage drinking session, away from prying eyes and their parents. As I drew my hand back up, it wasn't a bottle top, it was a ring, an old ring. Maybe twenty-five years old. I was still looking at it, lay there in the palm of my hand, when my phone started ringing. I dropped the ring into my pocket. Maybe I'll post it on social media, to see if I can find out who has lost it and then return it to its rightful owner.

I grabbed my phone again and swiped along to answer. "Hello"

"Hi Connor, it's John" came the voice back.

"I know who it is, your name came up when you rang, what's up?" I've known him for ten years and we always start the conversation in the same way, every time.

"Are you still at your friends? The one whose wife is on those tape?"

"No, I left about five minutes ago. Listen, if she's in trouble it can wait until the morning and whatever it is, Jonny had nothing to do with it. Ok!" I need to keep this guy in check.

"That's the thing Connor, it's Jonny that's in trouble, I've just finished with the tapes, and she paid to have him killed, Ben Stapleton was the wrong man, it was supposed to be your friend that got killed. I've sent a car over to the house, but I don't know how long it will take to arrive" "Fuck, I'm heading there now!".

I began to run back along the riverbank. I tried to ring Jonny. No answer. Then I tried ringing Chris on route, he picked up straight away.

"Hey man, I hope this isn't you crying down the phone about me taking your money?" Chris was clearly showing off to the taxi driver. I was sober now, adrenaline coursing through my veins and not alcohol anymore. "Can you get back to Jonny's right now?"

"Why would I do that, plus Beth will be there, I could do without seeing her this week" Chris replied. "Listen, Jonny's in trouble can you get back there now!?" my voice raising, and my speed picking up along the riverbank. "I'll give him a ring in the morning Connor" "No, get to his house now, I need your help" I was growing impatient, every moment he wasn't heading back to Jonny's, he was heading further away.

"But" Chris spoke, and I cut across him.

"But fuck all. Turn the cab around and get the fuck back to his house now!" I didn't have time to continue this conversation, I tried to ring Jonny again. Still no answer.

"FUCK!" escaped my lips to the sleeping trees and rolling river.

With my phone now back in my pocket, I started to sprint. I was fit enough to do that no problem. As the trees and branches flew past me, all I could think about was getting him out of that house, maybe not even out of it. But to stay with him and make sure he was safe until the police car arrived, with some back up.

I'd made it back to the bridge. No time to take in the scenery this time. I should be at Jonny's in a minute or two if I keep up this pace. I didn't look to see if any cars were coming when I crossed the road on the bridge. A bright flash of light and I went spinning over the bonnet, my back shattering the windshield as the screech of tyres followed. As the car came to a stop, I rolled off the bonnet and landed against the tarmac, face first. Struggling to stand, I heard the car door open.

"Shit are you ok, you came out of nowhere?" the voice behind me, distant.

"I'm ok, I'm ok" I didn't turn to look at the man, I prised myself off the road and started running again, I could feel and hear the glass from the car windshield falling from me, as my pace picked up again. I can't stop, I'll have plenty of time to rest when he is safe. I drew my hand across my brow to wipe away the sweat, I could feel it building up. When my hand lowered, it wasn't sweat, it was blood. I must have cut my head, pretty bad, as the blood was now running down the side of my face.

Almost there, keep going. If Chris had got the message from my phone call, he would be here soon. I turned into the street, I could see the lights on in his house. Sprinting towards him. I swung myself into the driveway, and up to the front door, screaming.

"JONNY, JONNY, JONNY" and smashing my blood covered hand against the door. Over, and over again. I could hear movement coming from inside the house. Thank God, he's coming to answer the door. Him or Dylan, it doesn't matter, I just need to get in there. No one came to the door. Again, my screams came.

"JONNY, JONNY, JONNY!" and the front door was now covered in my blood, like a house dressed up for Halloween. The noises from inside, were a mix of crashing and yelling. I started to kick, punch, and shove the door. It wouldn't budge. As I drove my shoulder repeatedly into the wooden door, to try and force my way in. I hadn't spotted the headlights of the taxi pulling up outside or noticed the sound of the door opening and closing again.

"What the fucks going on?!" Came Chris's voice behind me. I spun to face the sound.

"And what the fuck happened to you?" I didn't have time to explain to Chris, what the hell is happening.

"Kick the door in, for fuck's sake. He's in trouble!" Chris didn't need me to say anymore. The sight of me covered in blood and the splats of red now smudged across the door. Chris stepped up to the front door as I backed away, giving him some room. He was a big man and now he needed to prove it. I continued my shouting again "JONNY, JONNY, JONNY!" and with one kick in the right place from Chris, the door swung open, and the splintering of wood coming from the door frame, burst, and then cascaded down onto the hallway floor. Chris went into the house first, with me following just behind. We looked into the living room, and no one was there. The sounds of thudding echoing through the house. We followed the sounds that lead us to run into the kitchen and there was the most horrific sight I have ever seen. I have been on murder scenes before that were bad, but nothing came even close to this.

I stood there and saw Dylan raising his arm and sinking a knife into the chest of Jonny's still body that lay on the kitchen floor. While Beth was repeatedly kicking and stamping on his face and body. As Dylan's hand raised again once more Chris leaped forward and grabbed his arm, as Dylan turned to face him, Chris smashed his fist on his face. Blood, spit, and teeth fell from his open mouth. The knife fell from his now open hand. Landing onto Jonny's blood drenched t shirt. Dylan's body wanted to collapse, he was out cold, but Chris wouldn't let him, still gripping his arm. Chris repeated the move over, and over again. I was sure Dylan would be dead soon, Dylan hung from his grip, lifeless, as Chris didn't stop. Beth turned towards me. Her instinct was to grab the knife as she bent over to retrieve it. I saw my opportunity. Her hand gripped the handle of the blade, just at the same moment, my right foot swung through the air and connected with her stomach. Her body raised a few feet in the air and sent her flying back. As she was coughing and gasping for air, one hand on the tiled floor and the other gripping her torso. The blade had been sent flying through the air and was now safe from her reach, should she try to grab it again. I swung my foot again; this time the hit struck her face. I heard something break, either her nose or jaw. She spun around and lay on her back. Blood pooling around her mouth and running down to the tiles. She was unconscious.

I bent down over Jonny. Repeating his name and asking if he could hear me. As I held my ear to his mouth, trying to listen for any sign of life. Dylan's body came crashing to the floor, in a heap, next to Jonny. Chris had obviously had enough of hitting him, the first blow had done it. But in the heat of the moment, he couldn't stop himself from continuing the onslaught.

"He's breathing!" I shouted up to Chris, who already had his phone out and was ringing for an ambulance.

"Tell them it's a police officer hurt; they'll be here quicker" Chris just nodded. I grabbed whatever was at hand, to try and stem the bleeding. When applying pressure in one place, only let the blood flow quicker out of another wound.

"Fuck man, he's got a couple of minutes and that's it" looking at Chris, who had now ended his call.

"They'll be five minutes" he knelt on the other side of Jonny. After dragging Dylan out of the way. "We need to keep the blood inside of him until they arrive. You concentrate on his chest, and I'll stop the flow on his stomach" I was trying to remain calm and give Chris clear instructions, he needed that, and right now Jonny needed us.

Another minute went by, I kept checking on his breathing. It was becoming slower, and less rhythmical. Not long and those breaths will stop, I didn't tell Chris that, I needed him focused. As we held tight grips with cloth filled hands against his many wounds. Two police officers entered the house.

"Connor, what can we do?" it was Danny, I knew his voice. We'd been working together helping DI Morrison on the Ben Stapleton case. I didn't recognise the other officer.

"Danny, check on these two. We'll concentrate on him" as I bowed my head in the direction of Dylan and Beth. Chris shouted, "Fuck those two, let them die" I looked Chris in the eyes and said,

"If we do that, then we are no better than them" He bowed his head and stared down at Jonny.

As the two officers checked Dylan and Beth, both confirmed that they were breathing. I checked Jonny's breathing again.

"He's stopped breathing, help me do CPR. When I say so you need to blow twice into his mouth ok?" it wasn't a question to Chris, it was an instruction and he got it.

"Now" Chris tilted Jonny's head back slightly and blow twice. I started the thirty repetitions of chest pumps. Each time sending a little squirt of blood from his open wounds. We repeated the scene over and over. It felt like forever, but it was only for one or two minutes, then a glanced to my left and saw the green uniforms come running into the house.

"Let us take over" Both me and Chris were exhausted, I nodded a yes towards them and fell back onto my bottom. Using my hands to slide myself away from Jonny's body, through the sea of blood that used to be a pristine tiled floor and let these guys try to save him. Machines were brought in, and more offices arrived, I remained sat on the floor, now with my knees pulled up into my chest, watching as the shocks were delivered to Jonny's body. The repeated sounds of "Clear" then another shock. It was over for him, and I'd failed my friend, I couldn't save him. Then the words rang in my ear

"We have a pulse".

# CHAPTER 18
# DAWN

Eyes closed and watching the pumps of blood flowing through the inside of my eyelids. It looked like a road map of Britain. Veins branching off in various directions like country lanes. A subtle whisper of my name "Jonny, Jonny" heard only faintly, as the blood continued to flow along those lanes. Unable to think straight. Could I be dead? If I was dead, then where are the voices coming from? And why could I now feel a little pain? The pain had gone when I closed my eyes the last time. So why had it now decided to return? Think of something, anything. Just think. Try and wake yourself up. Concentrate. Small steps, that's all you need to do for now. My hands, think about your hand. Clench a fist, just do something. When I thought about closing my hand into a fist, a flash of light shot across my eyes. It was Dylan's face. Dylan as a child. On that roundabout in the park. Facing me, that huge smile across his face. My hand closed, gripping onto the bar that separated us, while we span around. Then the flash was gone once more, and my hand wasn't gripping the bar. It was softer than that and warm to the touch. It was a hand. But who's hand, my eyes still wouldn't open. Where am I? whose hand am I holding? It must be Beth's hand. It was slight and not small enough to be a child's hand but small enough that it must be a woman's hand.

I lay there holding onto her hand for hours, drifting into the unknown and then back again. I could hear my name again "Jonny, Jonny" it was louder than before and then I could hear sports commentary of a football game that hadn't been played yet, a game that shouldn't be played for another month. The words passed by me, and a hand was placed on top of mine. "Please open your eyes" came the voice again. Come on, you can do it. I thought to myself, you already moved your hand, and your eyelids are a lot smaller. The flash of light came again. This time it wasn't from a memory. It was from my will to open those eye lids. A will to see where I was, a will to see whose hand I was holding. The light burned my eyes "slowly does it" came from the unknown. My mind now becoming impatient. Come on, just opening your eyes. The burn continued for a few moments, while I tried to adjust. I could see, but not very clearly. I could see the white bedding, draped over my legs, neatly tucked into my sides. I'm in my bed and holding Beth's hand. As my vision became more into focus. The centre circular of sight I had, now doing that lake and water ripple thing. Clearing further and further, until the ripple ended this time on the outer rim of my eye socket. The TV was the first thing I saw clearly, it was a tiny screen and had the football on. These aren't supposed to play for another month, had I woken up in the future?

That TV wasn't mine. And this bedding was cheap and thin. Also, not mine. I also don't remember having a clipboard hung from the bottom of my bed either. Where am I, now starting to panic, I can feel my temperature rising, my breathing short and fast. "Take it easy, sleepy head. You're safe" as the sounds came to me, I turned and was finally able to appreciate the woman who's hand I'd been gripping. My breathing slowed down and when I saw her face. I know I was safe.

"Julie, where am I am?"

"You're in hospital and have been for the last four weeks boss" her smile showed on her face and a tear ran from the corner of her eye.

"How about you just call me Jonny?" as I gripped her hand harder and began to cry myself.

"Ok Jonny. How are you feeling?" her other hand, the one free of my grip, was stroking my arm.

"Tired and confused. I remember the night. But that's it" her hand left my arm and wiped away my tears.

"You need to rest, there'll be plenty of time to talk about it, when you're feeling better boss, sorry, Jonny" "Please tell me now, I'll hear the truth from you" she looked down at my hand and then up and into my eyes "Ok. Well on the night it happened. Connor and Chris came back and found you on the floor and those two doing what there were doing. They managed to stop them and stayed with you. Trying to keep you alive long enough for the ambulance to arrive. Then you were brought here. You were in surgery for six hours and then you must have fell into a coma and now you've woken up. You'll have some nasty scars on your body and one above your eye, but you're still a handsome guy. Jonny, you're very lucky to be alive" her tears were flowing now and the handsome comment, made me smile.

"I owe Connor and Chris a drink for this" she looked up at me "and I still owe you a drink to, although that might be in a few weeks" as I spoke, her smile radiated her beauty. She is my comfort blanket, and her husband is a lucky guy to have such a caring wife in his life.

"Do you know why they did it?" I asked Julie, but when I thought about it, Connor would know everything.

"Connor told me everything. They have been having an affair for years. I'm sorry. And the plan was to use your life insurance to pay for a new start for just the two of them. So, they arranged with Tommy Carters mob to have you killed. Twenty-five thousand up front and twenty-five when it was over. But they got the wrong man. She had told them the route you would walk home from the pub and that you were wearing your green coat. But you left that at Connor's house. So, when they saw Ben's khaki coat, they thought he was you. But Tommy still wanted his money, regardless of whoever's body ended up in the river". She was trying to deliver the information in a way that I could comprehend and so far, I was following.

"So that bitch made me pay the outstanding money for my own death, I dropped it off for my own funeral" that must have been why Frankie looked so smug when he asked me if she had told me what the money was for. "That's exactly what happened and those photos of her were all a setup, she knew that if you thought she was in danger, then you would do anything to help her. It was all planned out". I looked into Julies eyes as I spoke "I never realised that my life was valued at such as small a price as fifty grand".

"It isn't, the house is worth two hundred and eighty thousand, you had money in the bank, and I found out from Hannah at work, that Beth had rang to try and find out, what the death in service payments would be. Which is three times your annual salary. So, your life isn't valued at fifty grand. It's valued, to her at least for closer to six hundred grand. That's why she did it".

"I guess I should make the effort to speak with HR a bit more" she smiled when I said that.

"You are taking all this news very well, considering" her eyes never leaving mine.

"I always knew something was going on, maybe not to this extreme. But something. Plus, I'm safe with you Julie. I always have been" she leaned up and over me. Bringing her face closer to mine. As she planted a kiss on my lips, while brushing my hair back away from my brow. As our lips parted, she said,

"I'll always be here for you" and then she hugged me, carefully as I was still in some pain.

"I know, Julie. You are amazing" I return, taking a big breath through my nose and smelling her perfume. Looking over the shoulder at the sideboard to the left of my bed, I could see pictures drawn of a boy on a swing, being pushed by a man. That was me and James. Claire and he have must have been visiting me. It can't have been easy for him to see me laying here with tubes coming out of me. Claire will have only brought him once and saved him the heart ache.

She held me for what felt like an hour before I heard a knock on the door. And the familiar face of the men that saved my life, too keen and eager to enter the room and not waiting for the invitation.

"Come in, he's awake!" Julie shouted. As the guys entered and walked around the bed to the opposite side from Julie. That's the first time I noticed the drip in my right hand. Feeding me for the last month.

Julie said.

"I'll leave you boys alone; I'll pop back later" I still held onto her hand and looked at her again.

"Thank you for everything" I said. She smiled, nodded her head, and drew her hand away from mine. I watched her leave the room and close the door.

"How long have you been awake?" Chris's impatience shining through. "I don't know, maybe twenty minutes" I replied. Connor asked,

"How do you feel?" it must be the standard question to ask in hospital. Surely if you were feeling ok, then you wouldn't be in here.

"I feel like shit to be honest, but I'm still breathing thanks to you two" as I landed my drip-fed hand onto Connor's Chris spoke.

"It was Connor who saved you, I just followed his orders" Connor jumped straight in.

"It was a joint effort".

"Well thanks officer" Chris laughed at my comment. "It's DS Mount now" with a raised eyebrow and a certain swagger to his tone.

"Well done mate" was all I could think of saying. "Thanks mate. Did Julie fill you in on what's been going on?" "Yeah, she told me about the money and plan and stuff, so what happens now, Bibby, Dylan and Beth go to prison?" I looked at Connor and his head lowered. He didn't look at me when he spoke,

"Beth will be. But Bibby and Dylan won't"

"What?! He peppered me with stab wounds and he's getting off with it?" I could feel my anger growing. "Dylan killed himself, while he was on remand. They found him hanging from the ceiling" Chris said, as it was too difficult for Connor to find the words. My heart sank, for all of what Dylan did to me, his life didn't deserve to end that way. Connor spoke again.

"And Bibby is a free man. It turns out that DI Morrison is on the payroll from Tommy Carter. Bibby was spotted that night by you and the people that killed Ben, they wouldn't be reliable witnesses to state that they saw him, given they criminal records. But then you gave a statement, stating that you saw him running, that was the fuel Morrison needed to get him banged up. The confession he gave was sort, easily enough, by one of Tommy's men threatening to rape Bibby's sister in front of him and his mother if he didn't confess. And they were getting his fingerprints on the weapon, the night you saw him leaving Frankie's house. DI Morrison planted the knife that was found on the riverbank, the stupid fuck left his prints on it to".

"So just Beth heading for the cell then?"

"Just her for now, yes. Her trial is a while off yet, but rumour has it that she could get fifteen plus years inside. That could give you the chance to shack up with Julie". I glared at him. "I'm not her type" and my glare turned to a smile.

"Too soon?" Connor said, as we all laughed. Chris joined in

"On a serious note, you know she's been sat in that seat every day for the past month. Reading to you, talking to you. Trying everything to get those eyes of yours to open. And today she finally did it" I looked over her seat. Now realising that she was the type of woman I should be with. She was caring and fun. It's a shame we don't see each other that way and the fact that she is married to Ted, who is a great guy. I now realise Beth for what she really was. Some kind of adulterer who, first paid for someone to kill me, and when that didn't work, she had a good go at it herself.

I turned over to face Connor. Looking into his eyes

"Hang on a second. What did you mean? When I said about Beth going to prison and you said, just her for now?" Connor had a glint in his eye. "I have an interview with a suspect at the station in thirty minutes. We'll see what happens".

# CHAPTER 19
# CONNORS – THE INTERVIEW

I headed into the interview room, one medium sized table and four chairs, two on either side. Sitting on top of the table was the tape recorder. It's not like the interrogation rooms you see in the movies. All that good cop bad cop routine and one wall with a mirror along it, while others watch from the other side. This is a basic, Northeast police station, where we don't need all the fancy stuff, it doesn't change the outcome. I invited Danny to come along, more for experience than anything else. As he was pushing to move up to detective now. he'll get there at some point, I'm sure of it.

As we both sat there. The door opened and in walked Tommy Carter and his legal representative. Both very smart and very casual in their approach. No doubt that Tommy's lawyer only had one client, he'll represent numerous members of Tommy's unit. I have seen his face around the station a few times. As we started the recording, the usual things happened. Names were presented to the machine and the necessary cautions were read out.

"Now Mr Carter, or can I call you Tommy? I want to start off by thanking you for coming in today. I know you're a busy man" I calmly spoke.

"Mr Carter will do nicely. Now get on with it, I have a lot on" came back from Tommy, trying to hold the power within the room. As his hands rested on top of the table in front of him.

"You seem to have a pretty good alibi for your whereabouts on the evening that Ben Stapleton was murdered".

"Yes, yes, I was with my wife and a few friends at our house. You already know all of this". Again, Tommy came back with a curt tone.

"Do you love your wife Mr Carter?"

"Of course, I do, we've been married for thirty years. What's the point in this?" I was starting to get on his nerves, that's just where I wanted to be.

"Oh, there is a point Mr Carter, I promise you that. Does your wife ever complain about you not wearing your wedding ring?"

"I haven't taken it off for thirty years". His eyes never leaving mine, while he spoke.

"Mr Carter, you aren't wearing it today". His eyes dropping, as his hand slipped from the desk and out of sight.

"I took it off this morning to clean the sink at home and must have forgot to put it back on" he was becoming uneasy with my approach.

"Oh, ok Mr Carter I understand. Well, can you tell me why I found your wedding ring four weeks ago on the riverbank?" as I reached down into my laptop case and drew out a clear plastic bag. I held it up in front of Tommy. Making sure he could see exactly what it contained.

"Oh, and before you try and think of any stupid responses. It's your ring because I asked your wife about it this morning when your weren't cleaning the sink. If that wasn't proof enough, it has you DNA all over it. Oh, and one last thing. It has Bens DNA on it too. Looks like you got your hands dirty yourself for a change". He had no smart words or cockiness about him now. His lawyer leaned over and whispered in his ear. Tommy took a few moments to compose himself. His eyes darting around the room and finally landing back to the plastic bag with his wedding ring still inside. A sheen of sweat visibly showing across his forehead.

Tommy opened his mouth, struggling to find any words to come out. Then finally said.......... "No comment".

I got the bastard.

"I just want to take this opportunity to thank you for reading my novel. Hopefully you have enjoyed it, I know I enjoyed writing it".

AH

Milton Keynes UK
Ingram Content Group UK Ltd.
UKHW030844190824
447134UK00007B/343

9 781803 819150